As a lady who likes to lunch
many lunc

The Gol
The Indians, with thoughts of Mary
Cousins, brother, and sister-in-law
The Sausage Club
College Gals

'One cannot,
Think well,
Love well,
Sleep well,
If one has not dined well.'
Virginia Woolf

ALSO AVAILABLE BY TERRY H. WATSON

The Lucy Trilogy:
Call Mama
Scamper's Find
The Leci Legacy

A Tale or Two and a Few More

For Children
The Clock That Lost Its Tick and Other Tales

ACKNOWLEDGEMENTS

This novella came about from suggestions from friends who felt that Julie's character in SCAMPER'S FIND, had more to say. Thank you, Liz Armstrong and Rebecca Forster, for inspiring this piece of work.

Sincere thanks to Christine McPherson for clarification of the manuscript; to my husband Drew, and to John Harold, for their earlier observations, and to Kim and Sinclair Macleod of Indie Authors World, for their patience and valuable support.

A CASE FOR JULIE

She stood defiantly in the dimly-lit hallway, staring up at the attic. The once rich damask wallpaper that covered the walls of the long passageway now showed signs of age, wear and tear from daily life, scarred in places where her children had played unaware of the value of the textured paper that they so carelessly bumped and scuffed. Unchecked by their parents, the children had enjoyed free run of the massive house; except, that was, for the attic. That remained out of bounds. The explanation that the floor was unsafe had satisfied their curiosity and kept them out of that forbidden room.

Now that she lived alone, she often took up a stance there in the hall, as if challenging the loft door to open and reveal its secret. She had to stretch her neck to see the dark opening to the hostile area. The light that had once lit up the passageway had long ceased to function, and left a gloominess that mirrored the darkness in her soul. What had been a regular climb now seemed to mock her, as the attic appeared to move higher and further from her grasp.

Only a few steps up the sturdy roof ladder, if only she could pull it down from its resting place, would bring her to the spacious loft. She longed to sit there one more time. It was now a monumental climb, one that she knew in her heart of hearts she could no longer attempt. But Belinda Harrison, a determined lady of strong character, was reluctant to admit defeat. Hand on hip and waving her walking stick in the air, she sighed as she called out: *Someday, someday, I'll climb up... but not today.*

She stumbled slightly and limped back to her sitting room. Her old bones restricted her freedom to move as she would have liked. She often gazed at the loft – unopened, unused since, well, ever since Ralph bolted it down with a determination that if they, in their old age could not access the attic, then no-one else would have that right. She could still vividly recall the day they sealed in their secret.

"There," said Ralph, his face flushed from the exertion of the completed task, "no-one will open that door without Herculean strength."

That had been many years ago. A lot had changed in that time – her children had moved away; her grandchildren, busy with their own lives, seldom called in except for the occasional brief visit which, as if by doing so, salved their conscience and fulfilled a duty.

"Catch you on Facebook, Gran," was the normal parting remark as they took off after a flying visit.

Facebook? Skype? Internet? All a mystery to her. Despite her patient grandson constantly guiding her through the mysteries of technology, she was still bamboozled by the entire system, afraid to click on anything for fear of blowing the confounded gadget, and herself, to kingdom come. The laptop, a gift from her grandson, lay untouched between visits.

Pen and paper. That will do me. Always has, always will, she said to no-one. She was a prolific letter writer. Her neat writing, once pristine, now showed a shaky hand, but the neatness, care, and pride still shone through. Letter writing was her main pastime now that her friends no longer called around to visit. She penned them as if nothing had changed in their lives, as if they were still alive. In Belinda's eyes, her friends lived on.

Poor Christine, she mused as she sat nodding off in front of the fire, *stuck in that home, unable to tend to her own basic needs and locked in a world of her own. Ellen, too, sent away from the home she loved to live with her son and his dreadful wife, all because she wandered away in that grotesque shopping mall and forgot her way home. A senior moment, that's all it was, but no, that daughter-in-law, what's her name, Cheryl or Chloe or something strange like that, used it as an excuse to have her move in with them so that they could sell the house from under her feet.*

"Are you sure we're doing the right thing by Mother?" asked the hen-pecked husband. "It seems a bit rushed to me."

"Oh, get on with packing, and put those confounded ornaments well out of sight. The housing market won't be as good as this forever. Make hay while the sun shines, I say. If your mother doesn't settle here, we'll have to look elsewhere for a place for her. I've collected some interesting brochures in case we need them," retorted the selfish woman.

Yes, letter writing for Belinda was a means of expressing her feelings, her regrets, and her hopes for her family. She wrote about her latest knitting pattern and her garden plants, her weekly trip to the lunch club, but never ever about her secret. No. That would remain forever locked in the attic. Gradually, the letters ceased to be sent, as one by one her elderly friends passed away. She continued writing, though, and placed the neatly folded sheets of paper in an envelope, addressed them, then stored them carefully in a tin box which sat beside her fireside chair.

She stood once more in the hallway as if something was enticing her there, drawing her back into a past long gone; a past where promises were made and where secrets were kept. She gazed at a long pole meant for pulling the loft ladder down – a heavy wooden pole fashioned by Ralph many years ago, and placed in a corner, never to be used. She dragged a chair across the torn carpet, positioned it under the loft door, and looked up, wondering how far she could reach *Silly old fool*, she chided as she dragged the chair away, *and you'll end up breaking your neck. Leave well alone.*

She and Ralph had make a pact never to reveal the secret of the attic. And he had taken that secret with him to his grave. As she held his hand, his last exhortation to her was, 'Remember our promise, never to tell.' And she would do likewise. Who was there anyway among her selfish children to have any interest in the past, in the history of the house, of life as it has been before they were born? They would not understand the secret of the attic, nor why their parents visited it when they themselves were at boarding school. They had never asked about the loft; they were never inquisitive enough. She felt that she had reared two very self-centred children.

I suppose we did spoil them, and perhaps over-indulged their every wish. We could afford to then, and in a sense, it cleared our conscience about the attic. Whoever buys this mausoleum of a house when I've gone to my Maker will discover the secret. I'd like to be a fly on the wall that day! She chuckled as she settled in her comfortable armchair for the last time. *Yes,* she whispered, *a fly on the wall!*

∞∞∞∞

Julie Sinclair cycled furiously towards the post office to send off an important document. She propped her bike by the door and rushed in, grateful to see that there were no other customers to delay her task.

"My, my, Julie. Slow down or you'll have me all in a tizzy trying to deal with you. Now, what can I do for you? Another one of your manuscripts? I must say, I enjoy your books..." rambled Jessica Morris, who had overseen the post office for as long as anyone could remember.

"Thanks, Jessica," replied Julie, as she caught her breath. "Good of you to say so... Has Jack Denny been in yet to collect this afternoon's mailbag? I meant to get this off earlier. I have a deadline to meet."

"Don't harass yourself, my dear. There's plenty of time yet. Now, hand it over to be weighed."

Jessica Morris enjoyed a gossip with her customers. She was a source of all knowledge of events in the village, gathering and distributing the latest news, interspersed with her own opinion on the matter in hand.

"I see old Mrs Harrison's house hasn't been bought yet, and that's her dead nearly ten months. There have only been two people viewing it so far, and they were in and out in minutes. I have a good view from the shop and know for a fact that no-one else has been to view the property. They tell me that it's haunted. It's the oldest house in the village, you know. Who would want to share a house with a ghost? Gives me the shivers to think about it."

Julie smiled as the postmistress continued to chatter.

"Her family didn't spend much time clearing it out. A removal van arrived and took everything in a few hours. Looks like they tossed the lot, and didn't keep any mementoes for themselves. She had some lovely furniture, from what I could see, but it looked a bit old-fashioned and probably wouldn't suit today's generation. Such a shame to see a lifetime of living thrown out like that."

Julie turned to leave, but Jessica hadn't finished.

"Whoever buys that house will have a lot of work to do. It will need a complete renovation to make it habitable. I once had a peek inside when I delivered a parcel to her. The hall looked dreadfully dark, and there was a musky smell when she opened the door...mind you, that could have come from the old dear herself. Apart from the huge garden, there'd be the loft and garage to clear out, too. I often saw a light on in the attic when her husband was alive. They seemed to use it regularly for something or other, but since he died I've never seen that light on. My bedroom looks right over to it."

"Perhaps he had a hobby, like model-building or something," Julie suggested. "Some men like to have their own space. Well, I must be off, Jessica. I've a lot to do before I head to a reunion with former school friends, and then I'm going down south for a bit of a break with one of them. I needed to get this document away before I pack. I'll be away from the end of next week."

Jessica Morris liked to have all the details; she had an obligation, or so she believed, to be a source of information for the community, and prided herself on possessing knowledge that no-one else had.

"What about the dogs? Will Liz look after them while you're away?"

Liz, a book critique, also owned the local kennels, where she and her husband homed rescue dogs. Julie, a dog lover, was one of their regular customers.

"No," said Julie, as she edged further and further towards the door. "Liz was at school with me, and she's coming to the reunion, too. But her nephew Malcolm, who helps at the kennels, will take my dogs over there for me. And he'll check my house while I'm away."

"Oh, I'll keep an eye on it, too," assured Jessica, as she waved Julie off the premises.

As she picked up her bicycle, Julie glanced at the old house and thought how neglected it looked, with the garden overrun with weeds and high grass. The wooden gate, hanging loosely by one rusted hinge, added to the general air of abandonment. *Surely the family could have tidied things up a bit before putting the house on the market*, she thought, as she turned for home with a final glance at the place. Her eyes were briefly drawn to the attic. She wondered what had gone on there that had so intrigued Jessica.

∞∞∞∞∞

Julie was looking forward to renewing acquaintances with some of her former school friends. She and Liz would travel together in Liz's car and, after the event, Julie was to travel south with another friend, Maggie, to spend some time at Maggie's country home, Chestermere Hall.

Unlike Julie and Liz, Maggie was not enthusiastic about the impending school reunion.

"Oh, Maggie, you must come to the reunion, you really must," exhorted her sister.

"Connie, I really, truly don't want to go there. I have no wish to renew acquaintances with people from school from all those years. I won't know many people."

"But Maggie, *I'll* be there, and there *will* be familiar faces. Both Julie and Liz are coming, as well you know. And you've already invited Julie to travel back with you. They are so looking forward to seeing you again. Don't back off now, please. It should be interesting to see how everyone has got on in the world, and it's going to be in a lovely hotel, *The Grand*, so you'll be right at home!

"And anyway, it's only a few days after Paula's wedding, so surely you can stay on? It will be good for us both to chill out after all the excitement. You and Jonny have been so generous with your gifts for Paula. The icing on the cake, pardon the pun, will be having her own chauffeur to drive her in your beautiful Bentley. My princess will be the envy of the town."

Maggie smiled. "It's the least we can do for our only godchild. But I'm still not overly keen about attending a school reunion. There are some people I never wish to set eyes on, ever again."

To appease her incorrigible sister, she promised to give it some thought, but in her heart of hearts Maggie knew she never wanted to face *them* again.

As it turned out, the decision was taken out of her hands when Jonny announced that he had to return to Parliament immediately after the wedding, since the Prime Minister had called an unexpected election.

"This snap election means that I have to be away to assist with the election campaign. I'm going to be caught up in this for a time. Darling, why don't you do as Connie asks? Stay on longer, and enjoy each other's company. God knows, you pair can talk! I'll fly down, and Jenkins can stay on and be here to drive you in the Bentley to your posh event. Connie will love it, and Jenkins can spend some time with his relatives when he's not required to drive."

Maggie knew it made sense, and it would be lovely to spent time with her sister. Connie, three years younger, was in many ways much more confident and outgoing than she had ever been. Connie's personality shone from a genuine interest in people and a voracious love of life. No-one could recall her ever being unhappy; her smile could transform the gloom of any soul. She had been extremely popular in school and her *joie de vivre* never wavered. No wonder she longed to meet up some of her old friends.

Connie screamed with delight when Maggie phoned to say that she would indeed attend the reunion.

"Reluctantly, darling, quite reluctantly," Maggie reminded her, "but I'll be there."

In the run-up to Paula's wedding, Maggie tried to concentrate on her god-daughter's big day and to put the impending reunion to the back of her mind, but to no avail. It brought back memories that she would rather forget. These resurfaced with a vengeance, causing her sleepless nights and a rather cross husband who hated being disturbed by her tossing and turning.

From an early age, Maggie's time at school had been dreadfully unhappy. She was an outsider, as her family had recently moved into the area. She had no friends; no-one to guide her through the world of a large school, when she had been used to the comfort of a one teacher school on a remote island. Her accent was different; her country clothes were ridiculed; she was isolated. She was the last to be chosen for team games, the rules of which were a mystery to her, and became the butt of everyone's jokes and the target of hurtful name-calling Margaret Piggott became, in the eyes of her foes, an opening for Maggie-Piggy to be her given name.

Why do children have to be so cruel? She had often wondered, as she longed to be back in the safety of her island classroom where learning had been fun, and hard work rewarding. Bullying was a new experience for her; it was something she had never experienced before. But here, she was slyly kicked, spat upon, prodded, poked, tripped up, and generally treated as an outcast. She had to run the gauntlet of blows, and race home at the end of the school day at the speed of light to avoid her assailants. Maggie's school life was miserable.

It came to a head one day in class when the children were engrossed, or should have been, in writing essays. Pellets dipped in ink were fired at Maggie. The teacher, too busy with correcting work, did not notice the discomfort and distress of his newest pupil. One of Maggie's most redeeming features was her long, waist-length hair; her crowning glory, as her father called it. She loved when it hung loose around her shoulders and she could flick it from her face with the toss of her head. To make it more practical for school, her mother pleated it and adorned it with coloured ribbons.

"Margaret," she would say, "you leave here each day with two matching ribbons, and for the life of me I never see them again. You are always losing one, aren't you? Try to be more careful, dear."

Maggie could not tell her mother that the ribbons were taken from her by painful tugs, leaving her eyes watering that led to more taunts of 'cry-baby'. She felt she had to endure the suffering alone. Her only solace was in coming home to the warmth of her family and to her little sister, whose smile and chat helped her forget her troubles...until the next day.

In class, Maggie was concentrating on writing. She prided herself on the neatness and gently curved italic-style that she had been taught in her previous school. Suddenly, she heard giggling behind her and felt a tug at her hair. Before she knew what was happening, one of her beautiful pleats had been cut off and lay in a heap on the floor. A few giggles turned to gasps; an eerie silence loomed, only to be broken by a scream. Maggie never knew that she could make such a noise.

Mr Taylor lumbered from his comfortable chair to investigate the screeching, which reached a crescendo as the child ran from the classroom clutching strands of hair. What happened in that room in the immediate aftermath, one can only surmise. Maggie ran home thinking that her lungs would burst before she reached sanctuary. She threw herself into the arms of her astonished mother, and dropped what was left of the hair pleat onto the kitchen table.

The next few days were a haze of blurred sorrow. Maggie remained at home, her family administering to her with tenderness, knowing that her little heart was broken.

"Your hair will grow again, sweetheart. It will be beautiful again," consoled her mother.

"I hate long hair," she sobbed. "I want it cut short."

Her father, now aware of the full extent of his daughter's terrorised existence, stormed into school and, had it not been for the intervention of the caretaker, would have torn Joe Haynes limb from limb. The obnoxious bully had been hauled before the head teacher, severely dealt with, and removed from the school building by the scruff of the neck by his overbearing father. The mortified boy had to endure the entire school, it seemed, witnessing his fall from grace.

It had been agreed that, as school was about to break up for the summer holidays, Maggie should remain at home and take time to recover from her ordeal.

"If only the girl had confided in me or one of the staff, we could have put an end to the bullying," the head teacher told Mr. Piggott, as they discussed the child's plight.

"Or in us, her parents," her father replied in his lilting

accent, which had taken on a roughness of suppressed fury. "Unfortunately, our Maggie is not one to make a fuss about anything, and suffered in silence."

∞ ∞ ∞ ∞

The summer passed idyllically as Maggie and her mother, with Connie in tow, returned to their beloved island to spend time with her grandparents. The freedom to run and play, explore caves and beaches, swim in the chilly waters, indulge in rock pooling, all helped to heal her tortured soul. They sat outside the croft and watched the sun set over the neighbouring island, lighting the area with the afterglow.

On the evening before their departure, Maggie sat with her grandparents pleading with them to let her stay there.

"Margaret, dear," explained her grandfather in his calm voice, "there's nothing here for clever girls like you and Connie. The big city has opportunities that you could never have here. Education in the big high school, when you reach that stage, will set you up for whatever dreams you have. God knows, we hate to see our young people leave the island, but that's the way of it. Always has been. Youngsters leave, many never return except for holidays, very few return to give anything back to the island. You'll be able to go to the big university, if you've a mind to. Your father had to leave, too, to find work in the big city to provide for his family. Crofting in this area doesn't pay enough for a family to live on. No, Margaret, it is not sensible for you to remain here, as much as we would love to have you around us."

"And we're always here at holiday time," consoled her grandmother. Maggie detected a tear in the older woman's eye.

Life after that summer took on a routine of school exams and more and more study, which Maggie embraced with an enthusiasm that surprised even herself. She loved to study. She now had a new friend – a young, enthusiastic teacher by the name of Kim Mathieson, who, aware of the past trauma, treated her with kindness and encouraged and helped develop her protégé along the road to her chosen career, that of a writer.

Maggie's wish was to attend university to study literature. It was to Miss Mathieson that she owed her love of books and consequent career choice. Of her former classmates, she saw little. She detected a subdued guilt from some. Attempts by others to befriend her by offering sweets and invites to join in their games, failed to win over Maggie's attention. Of Joe Haynes, she saw even less. He had been moved to another class. On the few occasions when their paths crossed, he lowered his head in shame and hurried on.

Maggie's remaining years at school seemed to pass quickly. Her wise grandparents had been right; the city provided opportunities which would have been denied to her had she stayed on the island. The best of these was the library. Maggie spent so much time there that Tess Devlin, the librarian, would often remark on it.

"Back again, young lady? You must have read every book in this library. We might have to order new stock to keep up with you," she laughed.

Maggie also had the company of Connie, and had no need to run home scared out of her wits at the prospect of a beating from her peers. Connie's loveable personality won the younger sister many friends and favours, leaving Maggie free to concentrate on her studies and to develop friendships that were to last throughout her life.

Life moved on, and Maggie continued her education at the local high school. Over time, two new pupils arrived –

Liz and Julie, who sat near her in class. They also shared a love of reading and the trio would often exchange books, comparing their merits like the professional critiques they believed themselves to be. This was to stand them in good stead for their future careers.

These memories encroached on Maggie's mind as she travelled to the dreaded school reunion. The rain had been relentless, and there was more was to come; it pounded on the windows in time, she felt, to the pounding beat of her heart. Connie was in her element, lounging back and enjoying the luxury that Maggie now took for granted. She patted the Bentley's soft leather seats, enjoying the breath-taking quietness of the ride as she investigated the mini-bar between the two seats.

Maggie had been dating Jonny Watkins for fourteen months before she discovered that he was in fact, the Rt. Honourable Jonathan Andrew Sinclair Smythe-Watkins, who, on the death of his father, had inherited not only an obscene amount of money, a vast estate, and rare paintings, artefacts, and antiquities, but also property in London.

He had previously met her family, and even travelled with her to meet her island grandparents.

"You have a fine young man there, Margaret," said her grandmother, as they walked together down by the shore. "Grandfather and I agree that he is very suited to our darling girl. That is, if you've a mind to spend your life with him. But what does he do for a living? He said he ran a large estate and was interested in politics. Would that be correct, dear?"

"Oh, Gran, I really do want to spend my life with Jonny. I've never been so sure of anything in my life."

Unsure at that point of his exact role in life, Maggie agreed that he did indeed aspire to be a parliamentarian, and that he had some connection with a country estate. Their love was all that mattered to her; his job, whatever it entailed, was unimportant.

On the verge of proposing, Jonny finally came clean, and catapulted Maggie into a world of opulence and luxury beyond her wildest dreams.

Their wedding was a spectacular event, and they married in the private chapel on his country estate, with close family and friends in attendance. Connie, Julie, and Liz were by her side as bridesmaids. Jonny had also arranged for Maggie's grandparents and parents to travel there in luxury; they were amazed and delighted at Maggie's good fortune, and knew that in Jonny she had found her soulmate. Her grandparents had never left the island, and were awestruck at the world beyond their safe environment.

Jonny's sister, Hermione, flew in from Australia with her cattle rancher husband and college son. Maggie was welcomed into the family with enthusiasm, and in Hermione she made a friend for life.

"I always worried about Jonny," she said, "in case he was taken in by some money-grabbing female, but he has chosen well in you, my new sister. My parents would have approved wholeheartedly of their daughter-in-law. I only wish they could have been here to see their son wed. My mother died far too young, from cancer, and Father soldiered on like a lost soul. He never really recovered from losing her, and the heist all those years ago still rankled with him.

"Did Jonny tell you about that?" Hermione asked. "I'm convinced that it contributed to his death so soon after Mother. I think death came as a welcome relief to him in the end, he just wanted to be with Mother. Oh dear, Maggie, you mustn't think I'm being morbid, but being home brings back so many memories."

"This will always be your home, Hermione," Maggie assured her, "and I hope you will visit as often as you can. Jonny has promised me a trip to Australia and, yes, he mentioned the heist but didn't go into much detail about it. It seems to upset him to talk about it."

"We were quite young and at boarding school when it happened. Our parents came home from holiday to find that the house had been ransacked and several rare and irreplaceable items had been stolen. My father was most upset that *his* father's war medals had been taken; he had been so proud of them. The strange thing was, Maggie, the stolen items were all quite small and easy to transport, so it would have been possible for someone in a car or small vehicle to remove them without suspicion.

"There were several staff here at the time, but no-one saw or heard anything out of the ordinary. We often wondered if it was an inside job, but our staff were trusted members and were almost like family. One of the items – a cameo brooch – was found in a jeweller's shop in London. A man had brought it in to sell, and was asked to return later to discuss a price once the jeweller had time to value it. He never returned, probably because the shop owner asked too many questions, as he realised it was a rare piece.

"It was eventually returned to my mother, but she never wore it again; she said that it felt contaminated. No other items were ever located, and the thief was never identified. My parents were told that in all probability the items had been spirited abroad. Father took it all quite badly."

After their wedding, Jonny and Maggie settled into a blissful life together. Maggie, able to indulge her passion for writing, could work undisturbed for hours on end while Jonny took his seat in the House of Lords. Their two children arrived in quick succession, and were the joy of their lives.

But now, she was about to relive a period in her life that had long been put to the back of her mind, or so she thought. The nearer they got to the venue, the more her stomach churned and rumbled. Had it not been for the delight on Connie's face as they drove along, she would have had no hesitation in ordering Jenkins to turn back.

She was jolted from her reveries by the chauffeur announcing their arrival.

"It looks like the storm they predicted for later is about to start, milady. I'll be here in the car park should you wish to leave early."

I swear that man can read my mind, she thought to herself.

He was a most considerate, pleasant staff member who had worked for Jonny's father from a young age, learning the workings of the estate as he grew from a young man to be the trusted servant he now was. He had no wish to retire, and the family were delighted to have his reassuring presence in their lives.

The storm he predicted was nothing like the storm raging within Maggie. All her old fears returned as they entered the hotel, and she took a deep breath and held onto Connie's arm.

The oval dining area was beautifully decorated: the walls were off-white, with sleek, white curtains with just a hint of colour; the chair covers picking up the shade of the curtain border. Chandeliers gave a luxurious ambience to the room settings. The venue looked stunning, and drew gasps of delight from the guests.

In the end, the evening went better than Maggie had dared hope for. She shared a table with Connie and her husband Norman, who arrived later having attended a business meeting; Liz and her husband Colin; Julie; and two of Connie's friends. They all commiserated with Julie on the end of her long relationship with her partner, Craig.

"We just drifted apart," she explained. "He worked away from home in the oil industry, and we seldom saw each other. He would often arrive home when I was at a crucial part in writing and he didn't appreciate my work.

"'Can't you do that later?' he would say, as I struggled to meet deadlines. When he was sent by his firm to the Philippines, I knew that would be the end of our relationship, and I was right. He met and married a lady from there, and they now have a child. He wrote an endearing letter, and I've accepted things for what they are. We will always be friends. Enough about me, let's eat. I'm starving!"

Even though they hadn't been together in years, there was an instant rapport among them. Liz was a book critique; her husband, a travel writer. And Julie, like Maggie, was a writer. In fact, the evening was so pleasant that Maggie's fears had all but been forgotten. It was such a delight for her to meet like-minded people and exchange experiences and opinions. And Connie's exuberance, along with her husband's sense of fun, added to the enjoyment of the event.

Before they knew it, the evening was drawing to an end. The vote of thanks having been given, everyone mingled for a last chat. Laughter filled the room as people recognised classmates and reintroduced themselves; friendships were renewed; promises were made to keep in touch; and tales of the past years exchanged.

Maggie was vaguely aware of some people hovering around her. She turned to find a rather grotesquely obese man, who had obviously over-indulged in the evening's fine wines and other alcoholic drinks. His appearance was unkempt. He had, it appeared, made little or no effort to dress for the occasion; his hair was dirty and matted; his ill-fitting shirt bulged to reveal a stomach, which was best kept under wraps. Days of stubble covered his bloated face.

Maggie wondered why he sought her attention.

"Maggie," he began, his words slurring as he struggled to stay upright. "I mean, Lady Margaret. Do you remember me? I was in your class for a short time. I hear you've done well for yourself. You're looking beautiful as usual, if you don't mind me saying so. Who would have thought Maggie Piggott would marry into the gentry?"

Suddenly, the penny dropped. She was looking at her vile foe, the horrid person who had made her life a misery.

"Do you remember me, then, your ladyship? Joe Haynes."

Maggie smiled but remained silent. The unkempt man chatted on, so inebriated was he that he thought her smile was an invitation to form a friendship. He swayed as he held onto the back of her chair, and Maggie recoiled slightly as his breath overpowered her.

"I hear your boy is into computers. Maybe he could pop over to my place...still live in the same flat, number 5A, and see if he can fix my computer. It's a bit sluggish now. Tell him to knock on the door and walk in. I never lock it, nothing worth stealing," he laughed. "Ever since my wife Winnie took up with some creep and left me without a stick of furniture, I live a simple life. Can't do much else on government hand-outs. It would be nice to meet your boy. I follow everything about you and your family. Do you remember Winnie? Winnie Slater? She was my pal at school. She's in a bad way with the cancer. I go over to see her in the hospice... well, for auld time's sake; she had no-one else. The creep of a man she went off with abandoned her when he found out about her illness. How can one human being treat another like that? Maybe you could go over and visit her one day...I'd make it quick, if I were you, she won't be long for this world. Did I hear your lass was a cancer specialist? Saw something in the paper about her. Maybe she could come with you to visit poor Winnie."

I well remember 'poor Winnie', thought Maggie, but remained silent as she recalled the nasty name-calling thief who regularly stole from her, the arm-nipper... *Oh yes, I remember.*

As he turned to leave, he patted her arm and said, "About that business with your hair...I'm sorry about that...just a bit of fun...no hard feelings then, duchess? Mind now, tell your boy to pop over any time that suits him."

As he staggered off, Maggie thought of her brilliant son, a rising star in one of the world's most profitable IT companies, now based in California and living the kind of life that she could only dream of at his age, and thought to herself, *I don't think so, Joe Haynes, I don't think my son will be crossing your doorstep...ever, nor my talented daughter, whose recent research as part of a team has paved the way for future cancer cures... No, Joe Haynes...never.*

Maggie stood up to retrieve her wrap that had fallen to the floor. It was picked up by a woman who looked vaguely familiar. She struggled to hold the wrap in her hands as her body shook uncontrollably, showing evidence of illness.

"Thank you," said Maggie, as she took the fur wrap from her.

"Don't you remember me, Maggie? I'm Jane Horton. I was in your class, milady, a long time ago. Lovely wrap you have there. Is it real fur? Looks expensive."

Maggie smiled and remained silent. She was facing another of her tormentors. Jane, the ink-thrower, the one who enjoyed tripping her up at every opportunity, the nipper, the ribbon thief who slapped her face. Oh yes, she remembered her well. The woman struggled to remain standing and swayed as she held onto her walking sticks.

"I'm not so well now. Suffer from Parkinson's, can't live on my own. I'm in a care home, council-run place, share a room with another patient who has dementia. I tell you Maggie, life is intolerable. If I had a bit of money, I could pay for a single room. I don't need much. I don't suppose, for old times' sake? It's not much..."

Getting no response, she staggered on towards the main door. Remembering something important, she turned back and said, "Do you remember my pal Debbie? Debbie Black? She died last year. Had a sad life with an abusive husband and took to the drink. You'll probably remember her, milady, we were always together. The drink killed her. Funny how life turns out."

Maggie smiled and remained silent. *Yes,* she thought, *I remember your pal. The name-caller, the pusher, the kicker. Yes, I remember her vividly.*

The storm had indeed become ferocious. Jenkins had parked as near to the door as he could, and escorted Maggie, Connie and Norman to the vehicle, sheltering them under a massive umbrella that he kept for such occasions. Inside, the Bentley was warm and cosy, and the sisters quickly climbed in, grateful to escape the elements.

"Well," said Connie, "you seemed to have enjoyed your-self, after all the fuss about not wanting to go."

"Yes, indeed Connie. I had a wonderful evening."

As they left the hotel driveway and Jenkins turned onto the main street, the storm seemed to increase in ferocity, throwing everything it had at them. The windscreen wipers struggled to clear the glass, and hailstones fell like cricket balls onto the roof. The car slowed down near a bus stop to allow a woman struggling with two sticks to enter the bus shelter which was already occupied by a bedraggled man. As the Bentley approached, the man waved, bent to peer into the car and almost fell on top of it. The struggling woman held him back.

"Aren't those the people you were chatting to at the end of the evening?" inquired Connie.

"Yes. Former classmates."

"Maggie, look at them. They are drenched. Don't you think we could give them a ride somewhere?"

Jenkins slowed down, and turned to look at Maggie for instructions. Outside, her two vile tormentors moved forward as if anticipating a ride.

Looking straight ahead, Maggie smiled. "Drive on, Jenkins. Drive on!"

Connie stared at her sister, her eyes wide open like a rabbit caught in headlights. "Maggie, what has got into you? Those people look as if they need help to get home. There's plenty of room here, I'm sure we could have dropped them off somewhere... Maggie?"

Maggie stared ahead, a secret smile lighting up her face. Years of torment were now put to sleep in one delicious moment. *Bully for you!* She thought, as Jenkins continued to drive. Amused at Connie's outburst, her stunned expression, and Norman's silence, he turned towards her sister and patted her arm.

"There's a lot you don't know, dear. I'll explain it all when we get home to your house"

"Well, I hope you have a good explanation," replied Connie. "I'm shocked Maggie, shocked... You of all people;

the most generous, loving person in the world..." Her voice trailed off as she turned her head to look at the rain battering the window. "Those poor people."

Later, safely back at Connie's house, the sisters sat together by the warm fire, clutching mugs of hot steaming chocolate. Maggie had to resist laughing at the scornful, almost enraged expression on the face of her normally easy-going sister.

"Okay, Connie, I owe you an explanation. This happened many years before you were of school age. We had just moved to the city from our island, and I started at the local school..."

Connie sat wide-eyed and silent as Maggie recalled her tortuous days at the hands of the vicious bullies. Her eyes filled with tears as she told of the hair-cutting episode, and shook her head in disbelief at what her sister had endured. She had been totally unaware of the events that had coloured Maggie's early school life.

"So, you see, Connie darling, why I was reluctant to attend the reunion. I admit to being afraid of meeting those people again, as it would stir up dreadful memories. But you know, dear, tonight has helped me put ghosts to rest. Meeting those two unhappy people and hearing about the others was a kind of healing for me. I have nothing but sorrow at their plight, but feel no obligation to assist them in any way. I must admit to a selfish moment of glee when I ordered Jenkins to drive on. I hope you understand."

Connie hugged her sister and assured her that she did. "How awful for you! And I knew nothing about it. I wondered why it was so uncharacteristic when you refused those people a ride with us, but I do understand. Poor you to have had such an awful experience! Now I understand why, when mother caught me looking a picture of you with lovely long hair, she ordered me to return it immediately to the cupboard. She was quite cross with me, and I was upset because I didn't understand what I'd done wrong."

"My school days weren't all horrid," admitted Maggie, "especially when I made new friends in Liz and Julie. They helped me over those dreadful times. Oh, and by the way, I'm meeting them for lunch tomorrow, we have so much to catch up with, and then Julie is travelling home with me for a few weeks. We're both excited about that."

The sisters talked long into the night, relishing the chance to be together, sharing their memories, hopes, and dreams for the future.

∞ ∞ ∞ ∞

Lunch with her best friends was a cheerful event, with talk of people they remembered and how they had fared in life.

"Who would have thought," Liz said, "that creepy Bill Minto would become a lawyer? He never seemed to do much work, and was forever in trouble for forgetting his home assignments."

Julie laughed as they recalled the lanky classmate who now looked much improved. "I actually didn't recognise him at first, and my mouth opened in surprise when Liz pointed him out. He looked a bit of all right, in my book. Did you notice that expensive suit?"

"Yes," said Liz," and I noticed the wedding band, so eyes off, girl."

After lunch, the two friends waved Liz off then settled in Maggie's car for the journey to her country home. The journey passed quickly; the quietness of the Bentley released in Maggie a calmness that she now felt, after her troubled feelings in the run-up to the dreaded reunion. Knowing something of the lifestyle of her adversaries was, she thought, retribution for their childhood actions.

"You're deep in thought, Maggie," said her travelling companion.

"Sorry, Julie, that's rude of me. I was miles away, thinking of our reunion."

Julie knew of Maggie's childhood experience at the hand of the bullies, and along with Liz had helped her through her remaining school days. She had heard, too, about the incident as the sisters left the reunion.

"Was it awful of me to drive past them on that atrocious night, when I could easily have offered them a ride?"

"Not at all, Maggie. You did what you felt was right, and it has helped put some dark shadows to sleep. Don't dwell on it. Put it in the past. They are sad people, but they chose to be what they are. They had the same education as we had in the early stages of life, but chose not to capitalise on it. Okay, I know family attitude and poverty have a lot to do with how we are guided in life, but I'm a firm believer that education, when taken on board, is the way out of poverty. Here I am on my hobby-horse," laughed Julie.

"Oh, here we are! Welcome to Chestermere Hall," Maggie said, as the car slipped quietly into the estate and along the winding driveway that curved towards the main door.

"The grounds look magnificent." Julie gazed at the manicured lawns and tidy flower beds.

"Let's have a stroll before dinner, to stretch our legs. I want to show you the new pond and summer house," said her hostess, "then we can chill out this evening and catch up on news and gossip."

It had been several years since Julie had last visited; life events seemed to have taken over, and before they knew it the years had flown by. They now found themselves approaching an age where they wanted time to stop and allow them to take stock of life. The reunion, despite Maggie's concerns, had been an opportunity to reconnect with friends – an opportunity that Julie had grabbed with both hands.

Relaxing in Maggie's comfortable sitting room after dinner, the two talked well into the night; Julie shared her writing success, while Maggie kept Julie up-to-date with family news.

"You are so lucky, Maggie, to live is such splendour. You're quite the lady of the manor!"

Maggie laughed with her friend. "It hasn't all been easy. The upkeep of the estate can be a worry for Jonny at times, and he is considering opening the house and grounds to tourists, to generate some income. The robbery during his father's time still rankles with him and, as custodian of the estate, he is quite wary of having strangers wandering around."

"What happened? I know you've mentioned the heist in passing, but was there much stolen?"

"Several rare pieces were taken," replied Maggie. "It came to millions of pounds in value, but you can't put a price on family heirlooms and treasures. It upset Jonny's father at the time, as several war medals belonging to *his* father, had been taken. He seemed to feel the loss of that more than anything. The elder Lord Smythe-Watkins had travelled extensively and brought back trinkets and rare treasures for his collection from all over the world. They each told a story. He had some magnificent antiquities, totally priceless.

"The strange thing was that the robbers took only small items and overlooked larger items such as some valuable paintings, which led the family to believe that a small vehicle had been used to spirit them away. Delivery vans and repair vehicles called regularly to the estate, so, if such a vehicle were used for the robbery, it would probably not have looked out of place. Seemingly, several country houses were targeted around a period of five years or so, and the only clue that linked them was some sightings of a work's van, white with blue writing. I think it had *Drained-out,* or something similar written on the side. As far as I'm aware it was never found.

"Would you like to see pictures of what was taken? The list was compiled for insurance purposes. Jonny never likes to look at it, but I think the pieces are spectacular. The insurers believe that the items have been sold overseas.

"Jonny plans to discuss the future of the estate with Robin when he is next home from California. After all, our son will inherit the estate, and Jonny wants his ideas on opening to the public. Our darling daughter, Letitia, is engrossed in her work and is happy for us to make decisions in her absence. There's so much to think about, like security of the house and visitors' safety as they wander around. The house doesn't have a lift to other floors, either, so that would be an enormous expense. There's a tremendous amount to think about. My feeling is that we should open up the grounds and gardens to the public and leave the house private, but that's not for me to decide."

"I wouldn't like to be the one to make that decision either," said Julie. "You would need experienced guides, and marketing staff, and people to run a shop and tearoom and loos; these would all be essential and expected by the public."

"And car park attendants," chipped in Maggie. "The list is endless."

The two friends, heads together, perused the pictures of the stolen items. Julie, in awe of the exquisite pieces, gasped as Maggie pointed out each item and described the intrinsic work crafted so many years before she met Jonny.

"I never tire of looking at this book of images of such splendid pieces. It's sad not to have them here where they belong. I guess they have long gone. My only hope is that whoever has them, appreciates the splendour of the items."

∞∞∞∞∞∞

Julie's stay with Maggie passed quickly, and she returned home refreshed and ready to take on her next writing project –something she had discussed with her friend. Maggie had only ever published some of her short stories in magazines, her insecurities from childhood preventing her from believing in her own ability. Despite Julie's encouragement, her friend had never felt brave enough to take the next step into the world of publishing. Her poems and stories were acclaimed in magazines, but, in her eyes, that did not equate as proper publishing, she had told Julie.

"Nonsense, Maggie, absolute poppycock. You are a fine writer, and you need to believe that." Julie parted from her friend with words of encouragement. "Keep writing, Maggie, keep writing!"

Back home, Julie dropped her luggage in the hallway and, after checking her mail and grabbing a quick cup of coffee, set off by car to pick up her dogs from Liz. As she drove through the village, she noticed a 'sold' sign at Mrs. Harrison's house. *Good*, she thought, *that house needs someone to bring it to life again.* She called in at the post office to collect a parcel and catch up on the local gossip from Jessica.

"There's a family moving in soon; parents, and two little girls under school age. I spoke to them...well, someone should welcome them, don't you think? They seem very pleasant, and plan to renovate the entire house before they move in. It's good to think that the old house will have new life."

As she approached Liz's kennels, Julie knew that something was different...very different. Silence. No sound was heard as she drove into the compound. Normally, the sound of a car approaching would set off a cacophony from the dogs – one setting off the other, as if competing to bark the loudest to warn of danger, or to welcome visitors who were willing to rehome them.

The silence was eerie. The former owners had kept horses, but Liz had converted the stable block into comfortable kennels for her growing brood of rescue dogs, and the area was normally a hive of activity.

As Julie stepped out of the car, the hairs on the back of her neck stood up, a sense of fear creeping over her like a veil shielding her from reality. Things were far from right. The paddock in front of the kennels was empty, save for the many activity toys strewn around the safe enclosure. Liz had filled the area with agility equipment that ensured the animals socialised through exercise and fun.

It was, Julie thought, like walking into a nightmare. At any moment, she expected Liz to appear with a family of dogs at her heels, yet she knew that her friend never walked more than three dogs at a time. So where were the others? Something was wrong – seriously, disturbingly, and frighteningly wrong.

She immediately headed for her friend's house, which was set at the back of the kennels.

"Liz!" she called out, her voice an octave or two higher than normal. "Liz, it's me, Julie. Where are you?"

The door opened at her touch, creaking a little for lack of maintenance. The silence frightened her.

"Liz!" she called again.

She heard whimpering coming from the back-sitting room and an almost inaudible voice replied, "In here, Julie. I'm in here."

When she pushed open the door, Julie found Liz curled up in her favourite armchair; she had obviously been crying for some time. Julie had never seen her friend so distressed.

"Oh Liz, what's wrong? What's happened? Are you hurt? Where are the dogs?"

Questions poured from Julie as she hugged her friend, looking for signs of injury. Liz silenced her with more sobbing, before wiping her eyes and, holding Julie tightly, began to mumble almost incoherently.

"They've gone, Julie...the dogs are dead, every one of them. Someone poisoned them. Oh Julie, I'm distraught...I can't take it in. Those beautiful animals were deliberately killed...your three as well. Max, Buddy, Rascal...all dead. Oh Julie! And the nine dogs waiting to be rehomed...every one of them, poisoned."

Liz could no longer speak. It was obvious she had been dreading having to break the sad news to her friend. She clung to Julie and let her tears flow.

As the enormity of what had happened hit Julie, she sobbed quietly. The two women sat together, holding hands as Liz, through gulps, explained what she could.

"It happened while we were at the reunion. Malcom had locked the dogs in for the night as he had been doing every evening, switched on the security lights and checked that all was well before he went home. When he arrived next morning...he was met by a gruesome sight; the dogs were all dead in their kennels. He had a dreadful, dreadful shock. Mr. Oliver, the vet, arrived with our local policeman – on hearing from Malcolm – and took charge of the most awful situation.

"Malcolm didn't want to disturb us at the reunion. He knew I would be home next day, and wanted me to let you know personally about the disaster. He's in a ghastly state, and blames himself for the tragedy. But it was not of his doing – he covered all the security checks, and left the dogs content and settled for the night.

"Mr. Oliver confirmed that poison was to blame. He said he had seen such a thing in another part of the county, but never in such numbers. He was quite upset, as he knew most of the dogs well. He consulted the authorities and they have established that the dogs had been given crushed chocolate laced with a high amount of antifreeze and some other poison... enough to kill them. Oh, those poor, poor animals..." Liz broke down again.

Julie could hardly take in the enormity of the situation. She wept with her friend, for the loss of her beloved pets, and for Liz's business that she and Colin had worked so hard to build up over the years.

The only sound in the room was the intermittent sobbing from the women and the gentle ticking of the mantle clock that seemed to highlight the passing of time, the passing of the animals, and the passing of all that Liz and her husband had built.

Liz looked as if she had been wearing the same clothes since she arrived home to the devastating news. Julie, always the practical one, took control of the situation, made hot drinks, and encouraged her friend to shower and change. Her hands shook as she performed the simple task of making coffee, and realised that she, too, was in shock. But she poured them both a stiff drink, made a quick snack, and sat by the cold log fire attempting to bring life into it, aware that life had run out for her beloved pets.

An inconsolable Malcolm spotted Julie's car and called in to face the woman whom he had long admired and respected. He wiped his brow with his sleeve, as his anxiety levels soared. He was a lanky youth, tall and slim but slouched, as if he had all the cares of the world on his young shoulders. Aware of his height, he carried himself tensely with his head down, as if by doing so he would conceal his stature.

Julie saw him approach and, aware of the young man's discomfort, reached out to him to console him.

"This was all my fault," he blurted out. "I should have stayed here instead of going home."

Liz and Julie spoke as one, as they consoled the youth and reassured him that he had done nothing wrong.

"Malcolm," Julie said, "this could have happened at any time, regardless of who was here. If some wicked killer wanted to do mischief, he would have done so whether your aunt was in residence or not."

Liz spoke up. "I do believe the poisoner knew that I was not here, which points the finger at someone local. It doesn't bear thinking about that one of our own community would kill those poor animals."

Julie, in an attempt to reassure the young man that she did not blame him in any way for the incident, suggested he help her tidy up the kennels and grounds, while setting Liz the task of putting her neglected home into some semblance of order. The house had clearly been left untouched since the disaster. In setting the task, Julie hoped that Liz might forget – even briefly – about the cruelty that had ended her dream of rehoming the animals.

She and Malcolm set about a clear-up of the area that had been left undisturbed after the removal of the dogs.

Julie shed a quiet tear when she stumbled across some toys belonging to her own dogs.

Finally, they stored everything in an empty garage and, satisfied that nothing remained to remind them of the horror, returned to the house.

"Now, Malcolm," Julie began, like a stern teacher reprimanding an errant child, "no more blaming yourself, please. You did nothing wrong. We have done all we can do here, so let's have something to eat before you go home. I don't think Liz has eaten much since this happened, and you look as if a good meal wouldn't do you any harm."

The three sat solemnly around the table eating a hastily prepared meal, the silence broken only by the scraping of cutlery on plates. It was as if the sound of weary human voices would open the floodgates and tears would flow once more. Liz, as if realising how hungry she was, almost bolted her food down.

Julie remained with her friend for several days until Colin returned from his latest travel-writing project at an international book fair. Although he had been informed of the carnage that had visited his home, his arrival prompted a deluge of tears once more.

"We'll get to the bottom of this, never doubt it," he said, as he comforted his wife. We have a business to run and I'm dammed sure that no thug will take that from us. All will be well, darling, at 'Safe Haven'."

Julie took her leave of her friends and returned home to a place devoid of noise, of fun, and the constant rattling of pet food bowls. She wept silently as she cleared the area that was set aside for her beloved animals. The room, empty now of their toys and dishes, blankets and beds, could not erase the memory of happier times. Bereft, Julie sank to the floor, curled up in a heap, and wept as she had never wept before.

News spread quickly through the area. It had been deliberately held back by the local PC until Julie had returned home to learn of her pets' fate. A buzz of disbelief filled the normally quiet village. Animal lovers kept their pets close by, and did not let them off the leash on walks that now became shorter and more hurried. Door-to-door enquiries were made, statements taken and studied, but no-one knew anything of the incident which had taken place at the rather isolated compound.

"I can't believe that I wasn't the first to hear the news," lamented the postmistress to her customers. "After all," she continued, "people depend on me to pass on what's happening in the village. Everyone comes in here at some point in the week, and they expect good service including local gossip, mmm, I mean, news."

Had Julie not been so upset, she would have been amused at the older woman's belief in her elevated position in the village.

∞∞∞∞

Life in the sleepy village of Yetts Bank took on a semblance of normality. Investigation of the atrocity continued in the background, with the local police constable keeping everyone up-to-date on progress.

"I'm sorry that I don't have much to report," said PC Bob, as he was known to the villagers. "The forensic guys have confirmed what you already know, that the poor animals were given chocolate laced with anti-freeze. It appears that the criminal, or criminals, disabled the security camera that Malcolm switched on before he left for home. There are ways of doing such a thing using infrared laser. Don't ask me how, it's too technical for me. As soon as I hear of any progress, I'll be in touch."

Liz, as a book critique, engrossed herself in dealing with several manuscripts which had been sent to her by aspiring authors. She and Colin had discussed the future and decided that until the investigation was complete and someone was held to account, they should not make any plans to reopen as a business. Colin removed the poignant sign from the gate. *Safe Haven* was consigned to the garage to await its fate.

∞∞∞∞∞

Julie, bereft now without her beloved animals in her life, concentrated on her writing while keeping a concerned eye on her distraught friend. On one of her visits to Liz, she cycled past the house that had once belonged to Belinda Harrison and was now occupied by new owners.

A young man who was working in the garden gave her a cheery wave, so Julie stopped to chat. She had already popped a welcome card into the letterbox.

The man, who introduced himself as Raymond Newton, thanked her for her card and continued, "I believe you are the local author, the postmistress pointed you out to me. Delighted to make your acquaintance. My wife is a great fan of yours; she has read all your books and was overjoyed when she heard that you lived nearby. Hold on while I give her a shout, she's in the kitchen."

A cheerful young woman emerged, wiping her hands on a cloth. Two little girls followed her, and stared in awe at the tall lady on the bike.

"Hello, I'm Mary, and these little scamps are Caroline and Lillie." The cute youngsters skipped happily beside their mother, and smiled shyly at the lady on the bike. "I'm thrilled to meet you," continued their mother. "I've read all your books and can't wait for the next one."

For the next half hour, the family chatted with Julie, told her of their plans for the house, and apologised for not inviting her inside.

"There's no space to move in there," said Raymond, "as we have boxes everywhere. I'm attempting to tidy the garden so that the children can have somewhere to play while we get on with the work indoors. Once we have the house in order, we plan to have an open-day barbeque for the village. People have been so kind."

Mary took up the story. "One kind lady handed in a chicken casserole – it was welcome, I can tell you – and another handed in some home-baking, and we have had lots of welcome cards. We are so glad we've made the move here among such kind folk."

"You've certainly taken on a challenge to renovate this house," Julie said. "I don't expect that the Harrisons did much to modernise it."

"There's still a lot to be done indoors, and in the garden, and we haven't even attempted to do anything with the garage. We'll empty it later, as it's not a priority. It looks full of rubbish."

"Yes" said Mary, "and then we have to tackle the loft. We thought of turning it into a playroom for the girls, but that's a winter project. There's enough here to keep us busy for months."

As Julie rode off, she thought how good it was to have new blood in the village, and looked forward to getting to know them better.

∞∞∞∞

Spring arrived with a flourish in Yetts Bank. From dark winter days, early flowers came into bloom in abundance and the gardens were a profusion of colour and perfume. Rhododendrons, from small austrinum to larger calendulas, azaleas, evergreen encore and hybrids, filled parks and gardens. The village had won the 'Village in Bloom' competition for the last three years, and committee members – keen to retain the trophy – visited neighbours, cajoling and advising them on making the show the best.

"Will it happen again, Tom?" Jean Greg asked of the chairman, when he called to deliver plants. "Will the black vase return?"

"Let's hope not, Jean. Let's hope the prankster has had his fun and will leave us alone. Your garden is looking good this year. Remember to keep watering these new plants, but don't overdo it. From what I've seen so far, I'm sure we have a good chance of winning."

Jack Denny, a neighbour of Julie's, rose early. His routine never changed; villagers could set their watches by their faithful postman, but not today. Events would change that. He opened his door and there it was. The black vase.

"Stella," he shouted to his wife. "Stella, it's started again. We have the first one, the first black vase."

A black vase full of freshly-picked azaleas sat on the step.

"Oh no, no," she exclaimed, and bent to pick it up.

"Don't touch it. I'll call PC Bob. He gave instructions to everyone that, should the vases ever return, they were to be left untouched until he could arrange for fingerprints to be lifted."

Julie, without her dogs to waken her with their playful exuberance, slept longer than she had intended and woke to shrill voices from next door. She rose quickly, donned a housecoat, and rushed downstairs to be met with a very distraught postman's wife.

"Oh Julie," Stella sobbed, "We've had the first black vase. It has started all over again."

Julie consoled the weeping lady and tried to put her mind at rest.

"It is what Jack has said, just some prankster up to no good. Try not to worry; it isn't serious. Someone is trying to frighten us and we're not going to let that happen, are we?"

"I suppose you are right, Julie, but...but, well, we all know the legend of the black vase."

"And that's all it is – a legend, a story, a tale. It's not real. It's like the books I write, fiction. It's not true."

Having herd of the arrival of the first black vase, Tom, the committee chairman, arrived with a few others and took charge of the situation. Several villagers had arrived to observe proceedings, including the postmistress who deemed it her job to close the shop for a short time to establish the ins-and-outs of the commotion.

"Now, everyone, please do not let this worry you. We know it's a bit frightening for the folks who find these darn things, but rest assured, it is a prank, nothing else. Someone is trying to scare us into withdrawing from the contest. Constable Bob has it all under control. "Ah, Julie," Tom went on, "I'm glad I caught you. I would like a word with you."

A shamefaced Julie replied, "I know, I know Tom...my garden is a bit of a mess, what with everything else that's been going on...I'll tackle it this afternoon."

"Good. You have some lovely blooms there at the side of the house, but they are going to be choked if you don't do something about the overgrowth. Look, I'll send some of the lads around to give you a hand. We don't want to lose the trophy now, do we?"

Suitably chastised, Julie went indoors to change and prepare for a day in the garden.

With assistance from the postmistress, news of the black vase soon reached the ears of the rest of the residents of the normally quiet village, causing concern, curiosity, and a modicum of fear. And a few days later, Kate Scott, working in her greenhouse, spotted on the back shelf a black vase filled with fresh azaleas.

"Oh no!" she exclaimed. Still clutching her trowel, she ran faster than she thought she ever could, to her nearest neighbour.

"May!" she hollered, as she stumbled into the woman's kitchen, "May, I've got the black vase. It's in my greenhouse. Come with me, please."

The two women hurried to the greenhouse. Their screams were heard by Timothy, the paper boy, who was delivering to Mr. Sutton.

"Timothy, run and fetch the constable. Tell him there's a black vase in my greenhouse."

The youngster raced off on his bike and returned with a rather breathless and out-of-condition constable, who bagged and tagged the latest black vase.

"I'll put this with the others to await forensics, although I fear we're not finished yet," explained PC Bob. "Whoever is doing this must have nothing better to do. It's a disgraceful waste of everyone's time."

Two more vases were found during the days that followed. And the main topic of conversation in the village was centred on the mysterious appearance of the black vases, as always filled with fresh azaleas. The past two years had shown a frenzy of activity when the strange event occurred. The first year, there had been five vases; the second year, six. Always, black vases filled with fresh azaleas. The short life of the beautiful flower ensured that the mysterious event happened for a short time only, as strong winds and early spring rain brought an end to the stunning display.

The local vicar found one in his vestry. He prided himself on his open-door policy where people could pop in for a chat, ask advice, or arrange for baptisms and other church services.

"Anyone could have left the black vase there," he told the constable, who yet again had to bag and tag the item while trying to reassure the nervous clergyman. "The last thing I want to do is to keep the church doors locked. It's a big part of my service to the community."

"That's the fifth one, sir," PC Bob said. "God help folk if we get to number seven. The folk know the legend of the black vase and are understandably afraid. If it follows the pattern of an increase each year...well...I'll have to ask HQ to send reinforcements to allay fears. It's getting serious. What with those poor dogs being poisoned and no-one held to account, I need some assistance from the Force. The community council have called a meeting for this evening to discuss the problem and to attempt to restore calm. They plan to set up a street warden group and take turns to keep watch. We have to catch this person, and soon."

That evening, the village hall was packed. Tom Carson, the chairperson, called for more seating to accommodate everyone who wanted to attend. As people bustled about rearranging the hall, a shout was heard from the store room where some men had gone to fetch chairs.

"There's a black vase here, on the store room shelf," shouted Alan Buckley.

"That's number six," shouted a frightened voice from the audience.

"Who is it meant for?" murmured another.

The chairman called for order. "Let's keep things calm here. It looks like it's not for anyone in particular; it's for all of us."

People became vocal, shouting out, some women screamed in terror. A sense of panic was beginning to ripple around the hall, and reached a crescendo of anxiety. Every-one seemed to talk at once, no-one listened.

"What if we get to number seven?" screamed an almost hysterical villager. "What then? We all know the legend of the black vase filled with fresh azaleas. The seventh vase means death to the recipient."

The chairman had difficulty in controlling the mayhem that followed. No-one was listening. Then one lone voice was heard to say, "Well, I'm not staying around here to be the victim. I'm off to stay with my sister."

Others too, began making hasty plans to vacate their homes.

PC Bob stood up and took charge. His voice carried authority. People sat down and listened to their popular village constable.

"I know you are all scared, but running away will only play into the hands of the person or persons who is trying to cause mayhem in our village, and take our attention away from the important flower competition. It's probably a jeal-ous rival from someone in another village, so let's keep calm here. I don't expect that the seventh vase will turn up. Do you or do you not want to retain the honour and the trophy for the best Village in Bloom?"

"Of course, we do. We've been working towards it," replied Jack Denny. "What I see on my rounds shows commitment from folks around here. The gardens are looking spectacular. I agree with the Constable Bob, let's not be distracted by a stupid legend. That's all it is, a legend. Let's win that trophy."

A murmur of consent rippled through the hall, as people settled to listen to Constable Bob speak. Order had been restored.

"The Chief of Police has authorised reinforcements in the form of a junior constable and a sergeant, who will live in the local guest house for the duration of their stay as there's no room in my cottage. Along with some residents, they will patrol our streets and be a presence in and around the village. They will assist in solving the dreadful crime, too, of the poisoning of those lovely animals. So, sleep peacefully in your beds. We've got this under control. Now, those of you who want to help keep the community safe, give your names to Tom here, and he'll organise a rota."

Calm was restored, and over the next few weeks, village life got back to some semblance of normality. The two visiting officers, Sergeant Burns and Constable Hart, duly arrived and were taken on a walk around the village by PC Bob to familiarise themselves with the area and meet the locals, before liaising with the community wardens. Seeing them patrolling the streets, making their presence obvious, reassured residents that all was well. Night patrols, too, brought a sense of contentment.

All seemed well in Yetts Bank. The seventh black vase was forgotten about...at least for the time being.

∞∞∞∞

The Newton family's barbeque was a great success. Almost everyone, it seemed, dropped in at some point to welcome the family, donate food and drink for the event, and to sample the fare. A children's play area had been erected to cater for the lively village youngsters, who relished the freedom to play while the adults enjoyed each other's company.

"You folk have worked wonders on this old house," remarked one man. "Who would have thought it would look so grand?"

"Thanks," said Raymond, "it's been a marathon task and we're delighted at what's been achieved. Next plan is to tackle the garage. From what we can see from looking through the dirty windows, there's a mountain of stuff in there. We can't find a key, so I'll have to prise open the rusty lock. We're not looking forward to cleaning up in there, but it needs to be done. I'll want to garage the car when winter comes."

"I'm up for giving you a hand with that," commented Jack.

"Me, too," said another neighbour.

"I can spare an hour or two," said Tom Carson.

Before long, an army of willing helpers had agreed to call around the next day to start the clean-up.

"I'll bring some tools," said one of the volunteers, "and we'll have that old lock off in no time."

Jessica, from her vantage point in the post office, supervised the mission in her own inimitable way. Whenever she had a quiet spell in the shop, she stood at the door and called over to the taskforce, sharing her pearls of wisdom and suggestions as to how they should proceed, all the time craning her neck to see what was inside the garage. She was less than pleased when Julie arrived with a bundle of parcels to be attended to.

"Someone has to keep an eye on those fellows," she muttered, as she weighed each parcel then stamped them with a ferocity that left Julie in no doubt that her interruption was unwelcome.

Suddenly, a shout came from the assembled workforce. "What a beauty! Let's get it out of here and have a good look."

Even Julie was curious as to what had caused such excitement. Finishing her task with a flourish, Jessica almost ran to the door and arrived in time to see that the men had uncovered an old van and were peering intensely inside.

"We need to find the keys for this. It's an old model; must be forty or more years old."

"Let's get the tyres inflated and get the thing out into the open," suggested an excited Jack Denny. "Raymond, have you come across any keys that might belong to the van?"

"There's an old tin full of keys, I'll go and fetch them. That's if Mary hasn't thrown them out."

Julie, caught up in the excitement, crossed the road to see what was attracting all their attention. Some of the men were trying to wipe off grime from the windows and from the body of the vehicle.

"Hey, it has writing on it," called a young lad, who rubbed vigorously with his sleeve to reveal what was there. "Here we have it," he shouted, "it's been a plumbing business I think. Look, it says..." he continued to wipe the side panel until he could decipher the writing, "*Drained-Out. Plumbers of Repute.*"

Julie, very quickly recalling something, called out to the crew, "Stop! Don't touch anything. Please don't touch the vehicle."

The men looked at her, startled at her outburst. But having the greatest respect for the notable author in their midst, they stopped to listen to her.

"What's the deal, Julie?" asked Tom. "What's got you so excited?"

"Tom, if I'm not mistaken, this van was used in several robberies many decades ago," she explained. "Trust me on this, please don't destroy any evidence. We need to get the authorities here. Can you cover it over with the tarpaulin again? I'm calling the constable."

"What? What is this to do with anything?" remarked one villager. "Let's get this vehicle out into the open. I can't wait to feast my eyes on it."

"No," replied Tom. "Hang on a bit. If Julie's gut instinct is correct, we don't want to interfere with evidence. Do as she asks, until the authorities decide what to do."

With two extra officers in the village to deal with the black vase mystery and the killing of the animals, there was no shortage of assistance when Julie cycled to the police station for help.

"What's the problem then, Julie?" asked PC Bob, as he and the sergeant studied the windswept lady who hardly stopped for breath as she blurted out her findings.

"Now don't think I'm mad, Officers, but I suspect the vehicle that's just been uncovered in the Newton's' garage was used forty or more years ago in several robberies in stately homes throughout the country. I know some people who had artefacts stolen. The thieves were never found, but sightings were made of a vehicle such as this, with *Drained-Out* written on the side. It surely can't be a coincidence. I've seen pictures of some of the stolen items. We need to follow this up."

"Now, my dear," replied Sergeant Burns, "let's not jump to conclusions here. Facts, that's what we need, facts. This is the first I've heard of an old vehicle turning up in the village."

Julie said, "It has only this minute been found in the garage. I came here as fast as I could to ask you to stop the men from destroying evidence."

The two officers looked at each other, each wishing the excitable woman would get on her bike and leave them to solve real crimes.

Sergeant Burns attempted to lead Julie towards the door. He was uncomfortable with village life, and was keen to return to the city as soon as the black vase problem was solved; he was reluctant to spend any more time than was necessary out of his comfort zone. He particularly disliked having to live in a guesthouse where the outspoken owner quizzed him mercilessly about the crimes that he was investigating.

He turned his attention to Julie.

"Right, my dear, you need to come back to the station this afternoon, its lunchtime now. If you are still in the same frame of mind, then you can make a statement and we will decide if this is something that needs to be followed up."

Julie had the distinct feeling that the sergeant wanted to brush this under the carpet, but her inquisitive mind would never allow that to happen. She shrugged her shoulders, drew the sergeant a look of disapproval, and left the office. She hated being patronised. Back home, she phoned Maggie and told her friend about the find.

"If my instinct is right, Maggie, this could be the van that was used all those years ago. I'll make sure that no-one touches it until the police have examined it, although the police here are reluctant to do much about it. They think I'm a silly, crazy writer looking for inspiration for stories."

Maggie laughed as she visualised her friend's encounter with the local bobby. Fortunately, Jonny was at home and spoke at length with her.

"If this proves to be true, Julie, then you have indeed made a marvellous discovery. I long to have my family artefacts safe with me again. I'll contact the Fraud Squad, who have the heist on file, and get their take on the situation. Give me the name of your village constable. I'll pass it on to the relevant authorities. I can't thank you enough. Imagine if this is true, right there in your village! It's astounding news."

"Let's hope that I'm not leading you on a wild goose chase, Jonny, but my gut tells me we are on to something."

Jonny said, "From what Maggie tells me, your gut feelings have guided you through life."

As arranged, Julie arrived at the local police office after lunch to make her statement. Sergeant Burns, the most senior of the visitors, interviewed her.

"Now, Miss," he began, "I believe you are an author? You spend your life making up stories, am I right? I take a dim view of people with runaway imaginations taking up valuable police time, especially when my men are trying to solve a minor crime or two in this place."

Normally unruffled, Julie took a deep breath and replied, "I assure you, Sergeant, that I am not wasting anyone's time. I, too, take a dim view...that is, of *your* attitude, when you have not yet established facts or properly inspected the vehicle. And as for dismissing the poison of twelve animals as a minor crime, and the mystery surrounding those vases that is causing so much upset for people, I am deeply concerned that justice will never be served in this village. And while I am in this frame of mind, I am not 'your dear' and I resent being patronised."

"Now, now, there's no need to take that attitude, Miss," he soothed. "Let's get your statement and see where it takes us. To begin with, how do you claim to know so much about these robberies and the supposed vehicle used in the crimes? From forty plus years ago, you say? That sounds a bit far-fetched."

As Julie related the conversation she'd had with Maggie, she knew that the sergeant was simply tolerating her and had no intention of taking things any further. His body language spoke volumes.

The young constable knocked on the door, interrupting the interview.

"What is it, Hart? Some other crime to report? Can't it wait until I finish interviewing Ms. Simpson?"

"It's Sinclair, Officer, not Simpson," said Julie.

"Whatever you say, Miss. Now, Hart, spit it out."

"Sir, there's a gentleman on the phone who wishes to talk to you, says he's Lord Smythe-Watkins or something like that. I didn't quite catch his name."

Julie smiled as the sergeant excused himself and went off to take the call, returning sometime later to the interview room.

"Hmm," he began, "sounds like I owe you an apology, Ms. Sinclair...hmm, looks like your instincts might well be right on this one...some Fraud Squad officers are arriving here in the next few days to inspect said vehicle...this could be a massive breakthrough for a case that always remained on open-file. I've sent the constables to cordon off the vehicle and secure the area. Hmm, as for the poison of the poor dogs, I'll chase up the investigation and assure you that I intend to solve this dreadful deed and that of the black vases. I'll go up to the garage myself and inspect said vehicle. I'm here to do what I can to solve crime, be they cold cases or new ones."

Julie stood up, removed her glasses, collected her belongings, and gave the officer a look which left him in no doubt that she was not one to be dismissed and patronised.

"I sincerely hope you do. After all, it *is* your job, and it is what taxpayers expect from you."

Suitably chastised, the sergeant headed straight along to the Newton's garage to see for himself what the fuss was about.

"It looks like this vehicle has been here for years," he said. "It's an old Ford 5cwt model, if I'm not mistaken; it looks in good condition, too, for its age. Cover it up and secure the area, Constables. We can expect the big boys here soon to tell us how to do our jobs."

He shrugged his shoulders, as if he wanted to shrug off the mysterious events of Yetts Bank, and turned to Raymond Newton. "Don't go near your garage, sir, we'll cordon it off, as it's a suspected crime area. Until we hear from the fraud and forensic people, it is out of bounds."

A buzz of excitement filled the village. Everyone, agog at what they were hearing and not having the full facts, allowed their imaginations to run riot and added their opinions as to what had happened in Yetts Bank many years ago.

"I was never convinced that man was a plumber," said one elderly resident. "There was always water pouring down from a drain in his garden; right down onto the road it poured, I tell you. In the winter, when it iced over, it was lethal. No-one can convince me that Ralph Harrison was a plumber. Sure now, wouldn't you think he would fix his own place first?"

Speculation continued, and rumours grew with each mention of the find of the vehicle. None more so than in the Post Office, where Jessica relished in imparting her views, be they based on fact or on her own imagination. Some days later, a truck arrived to remove the suspect vehicle to Police HQ, where it would be thoroughly inspected by forensics officers.

As they prepared to remove the van from the garage, one of the team spotted something lying on the floor of the Ford.

"Look, sir," he called to the supervising officer, "there's something here that you need to look at. It's an earring or pin brooch, I think, and it's covered in dust. Looks really old, like an antique."

"I'll bag it," replied the officer. "We may get prints from it – that is, once we have eliminated yours."

"Sorry, sir, I never gave a thought to my prints being on it."

Once the vehicle had been removed from the garage, forensic officers went to work inspecting the rest of the dusty garage in minute detail, bagging and tagging items as they went along. Mary, always the good hostess, kept the team supplied with coffee and cake, while shepherding her inquisitive children away from the banned area.

It was several weeks before Raymond could finally take possession of his garage, which was now thoroughly clean and ready for use. He and Mary had been overawed at the frenzy of activity and the startling find of the Ford vehicle.

"And we thought that we were moving here to have a quiet life!" said Mary.

"Yes, but at least we now have a clean garage to make proper use of. I'll replace the worn doors and we can use it for the purpose it was meant for. I'm keen to follow this up and discover the mystery of our garage. What else will this old house turn up?" he laughed.

∞∞∞∞∞

Julie had promised Liz that she would check her house and grounds while her friend and her husband enjoyed a short holiday – a welcome break after the dreadful animal killings. She rode along on her bicycle, waving cheerily to people she encountered on her ride.

Parking her bike outside the house, Julie used the key she had been given, entered the building, and had a quick tour of each room, ensuring that nothing had been disturbed and that whoever had poisoned the animals had not returned to make mischief. Satisfied that all was well, she ventured out to the kennels. A sadness filled her heart as she walked through the quiet tomb-like area, once a hive of activity but now a sombre, silent patch.

She sighed as she thought of her own three rescue dogs: Max, a wire-haired fox terrier – *more a terror*, she laughed to herself, as fond memories of the friendly and fearless eight-year-old came to mind; Buddy, her rather sedate, gentle elderly beagle, who liked nothing more than to relax in front of the log fire, dreaming dog-dreams of rabbit-chasing; and Rascal, her well-named shih tzu – a playful and lively four-year-old who reminded Julie of a previous dog that she once rescued from the woods where she often walked. *Rascal is so like Scamper in nature,* she reminisced.

She stood in the kennel area for some time, letting the tears stream down her face, and wishing that it had all been a dream and that at any moment her lively pooches would rush over to her, frolicking and jumping excitedly as she rummaged in her pocket for treats. As she peered over the half-door of each kennel, she spotted in one a small glass bottle glinting in the sun. Retrieving it, she popped the cork and sniffed at the pungent odour. *Oh, that's foul,* she thought as she drew back from the offending bottle.

Julie examined it for markings: it was a plain bottle, unlabelled, and gave no clue to its contents. *Could this have been dropped by the criminal?* Her inquisitive mind went into overdrive as she rummaged in her pocket to retrieve a paper tissue to wrap it in. Further inspection of the kennels and surrounding grounds did not turn up further evidence. She returned home, fully intending to take the mysterious bottle to PC Bob, but was side-tracked by a rather long phone call. *It's too late now to disturb Bob*, she thought as she settled to read by the fireside. *I'll call in tomorrow.*

She spent the next day engrossed in her writing. While she desperately missed her dogs, she was glad not to be disrupted by one or other of them demanding treats or walks or such like, and continued with her work, having forgotten about the glass bottle that had previously disturbed her so much.

Village life took on a less anxious pace. The presence of two extra police officers calmed the concerned residents, allowing a modicum of normality to pervade. The neighbourhood watch carried on as usual; Jack Denny continued his round of mail delivery; Timothy, the whistling boy, carried on with his paper delivery, waving and calling out to villagers as he rode his bicycle through the quiet streets; and Tom Carson resumed the serious task of encouraging villagers to make the best of their garden display.

"We have only a week left now until the judging takes place. Keep up the good work!" he encouraged them.

Jessica Morris, too, proceeded to serve the community, not only with products from the Post Office, but with snippets of any gossip that she could conjure up, while Julie Sinclair immersed herself in her writing. All appeared well in Yetts Bank.

The day for the judging of the flowers began with sunshine that remained throughout the day, giving a warmth to the area that showed the blooms at their best. Two official-looking judges, carrying clipboards, were accompanied by Tom

Carson and some other committee members as they walked around the village, inspecting each area, making notes as they went along. They whispered to each other, keeping their thoughts from the anxious chairman and his team. They took pictures of some of the hanging baskets, the village green with its profusion of colour, as well as several private gardens. They glanced at Julie's garden and moved on. In the evening, the villagers assembled in the hall to hear the outcome of the visit.

"Whether we win or not," said Tom to his committee, "we will put on a feast for everyone to show our appreciation for the effort that has been put into the display. Everything is ready in the marquee. I can't wait to get my teeth into some of the home baking."

People waited patiently as the two judges mounted the stage. Their demeanour gave nothing away.

"I fear it can't be for us this year," whispered one lady, "they look too serious."

"Look at their faces, not a smile to be seen. I think we've lost the trophy," replied her companion.

A hush fell on the gathered assembly as Tom Carson welcomed the visitors and thanked them for their time and effort. He felt nervous as he awaited the result.

The head judge – a formidable lady, dressed in a tweed skirt and jacket and wearing a hat, which for all the world looked like a flowerpot – adjusted her glasses and peered at the assembled crowd. She launched into a long speech about the various villages that she had had the pleasure of visiting, and mentioned how difficult it had been this year to select a winner.

"However," she began, "my colleague and I have decided that the Best Village in Bloom for this year should go to..."

As she adjusted her glasses and searched through her paperwork, an irate voice whispered loud enough to be heard, "Hurry up, the suspense is killing. This isn't *Britain's Got Talent*, get on with it."

Tom Carson glowered at the whisperer, showing his disapproval and hoping the remarks would not alter the result.

"The prize this year for Best Village goes to Yetts Bank, and I congratulate you all for such a fine display."

Her felicitations were drowned out by cheers and clapping. A beaming Tom Carson gave a quick vote of thanks and invited everyone to enjoy the feast on offer.

With the competition now settled, Sergeant Burns spoke to the local constable. "We have to get these people focused on the crimes that I've come here to help solve. Maybe now that that darn flower show is over, we can cajole them into concentrating on both crimes. Usually after a period of time when people have had a chance to recall, they come up with something that they remember. I propose that we visit each house again and talk to the villagers, get their take on things...you never know what might come from it. I'm anxious to wrap up these crimes and let everyone move on with their lives." *And let me get back to city life*, he thought to himself.

For the next few days, the officers visited each house, asking people to remember where they were when the various crimes had taken place and to share their suspicions, in confidence of course, as to who could have committed such disturbing acts.

∞∞∞∞

Julie, completely engrossed in her writing, had not been seen for two days and missed the commotion that caused great excitement in Yetts Bank. One of the villagers arrived at her house to impart the distressing news.

"Sorry to disturb you, Julie, but no-one has seen you for a few days and you've missed the latest news about your dogs. The police have made an arrest."

"Thank goodness for that. Who is it? Is it anyone that we know?"

The village messenger, unsure of the reaction he would get from the writer, quietly said, "Its Malcolm, Malcolm Kent. Julie, he was brought in for questioning by PC Bob and the visiting constable. He's with them now. I thought you ought to know."

"No!" exclaimed Julie. "That can't be right. Malcolm would never do such a thing. I'm going straight down to the police office to talk to the officers."

She stood up, donned her warm jacket, and stormed out of the house, leaving her bemused neighbour standing on the doorstep.

An irate Julie arrived at the police office, threw her bike on the ground and, breathless but determined, demanded to speak to Sergeant Burns.

"Sorry ma'am, but he is in the interview room and does not want to be disturbed. He is interrogating a suspect," said PC Hart.

"That's why I'm here. I wish to speak with Sergeant Burns right now. He has the wrong person in custody." Julie's fingers tapped the desk in total frustration. "The least you can do is ask him to give me a moment of his time."

"That's more than my job is worth, ma'am. I have instructions not to interrupt the interview."

"You can tell your sergeant that I'll be back, and that he has the wrong suspect."

Julie thumped the desk in annoyance and rode off, barely able to control her bike and her anger. She was determined to somehow or other help Malcolm, whom she knew was being used as a scapegoat. As she neared the Post Office, she heard Jessica Morris sounding off to a gathering of shoppers.

"Of course, I always knew that man was evil. You can tell by the eyes. At least he is in custody, thanks to me and my observation and good memory, after all..."

Her diatribe was interrupted by Julie entering the shop, her face purple with rage as she listened to the gossipy busybody.

"Stop that talk right now!" she said. "You people should be thoroughly ashamed of yourselves, spreading untruths and destroying the character of a fine young man."

As she spoke, Julie did not move her eyes from the face of the postmistress, who was having none of it.

"There's no smoke without fire," Jessica replied. "He wouldn't be in custody if he were innocent now, would he? After all, he all but admitted his crime to me."

She stood defiantly in front of Julie, challenging her to respond. The other shoppers, quiet now, watched the unfolding confrontation, unsure of whether to go or stay.

"What do you mean, he admitted his crime to you?"

"Near enough. He stood here in this very shop, blabbering like a baby, and muttering 'it's all my fault, it's all my fault'. If that's not an admission of guilt, you tell me what is? And that's what I told the constable. He believed me, even if you don't."

"You foolish woman!" shouted Julie. "You foolish, foolish woman. Malcolm was not admitting to any crime – far from it; he was blaming himself for not being there for the dogs. He had done all that was asked of him, and more. He fed and watered them before checking that they were settled for the night. He spent more time with them than he was expected to, and was feeling guilty at not being there when the killer struck. When he came in here, he was in shock. You are a silly, stupid woman to have told the constable a pack of home-made gossip. An innocent man could go to prison because of you, and meanwhile the real culprit is still at large."

Leaving the postmistress red-faced and rather subdued, Julie took off once more to the village police office where she found PC Bob manning the desk, the junior constable having been relieved of his duties to make tea for the sergeant.

"Ah, Julie," he said, "I heard that you had been in here earlier, trying to prevent justice being served."

"Bob," she began. "Constable Bob, there has been a dreadful mistake. Jessica Morris has misled you. Malcolm Kent is an innocent man, as you well know. You have known him all his life, he doesn't have a bad bone in his body. You have to get him out of here."

"Now, Miss, this is not one of your made-up dramas, this is reality. Some of us live in the real world, and Mr. Kent has all but admitted he was the perpetrator of the crime. By the time the sergeant has finished with him, he will have signed his confession and be held over to appear in court. Then we can all concentrate on solving the frightening case of those obnoxious vases. Now, I suggest you return to your job and leave the rest of us to do our work."

"Constable, all I'm asking is for one minute of the sergeant's time."

Realising that she could not change his mind, Julie rode off again, leaving the constable smiling at having rid himself of an interfering woman.

She entered her house just as the phone was ringing. *Now what?* She muttered furiously as she answered rather abruptly.

"Hi Julie. My, you sound harassed. Have we called at a bad moment? Colin and I are home and have left it too late to buy some groceries. I can't get hold of Malcom, he was to buy some things and put them in the fridge. We wondered about cadging a meal from you. Julie, is everything alright? You sound strange."

At the sound of Liz's voice, Julie kept her emotions in check and, as calmly as she could, asked Liz and Colin to come right away.

"Liz, please don't stop anywhere or talk to anyone, come straight here. Something has happened, and I want you to hear it from me."

"This sounds serious, Julie. We will be right over."

Julie set about preparing supper, throwing ingredients together, stirring, heating, and generally making a meal as if on auto pilot. As she set the table and opened a bottle of wine to allow it to breathe, Liz and Colin arrived.

"Julie, you've been crying. I knew something was wrong by your voice. What is it? What has happened?"

Colin poured the wine as Julie told of Malcolm's arrest and the part played in it by the interference of the local gossip.

"I'm going there now to see the officer," screamed Liz, as she sat her wine glass down. This is ridiculous. Colin, come with me. Julie stay here and cook, it will keep you busy. Set a place for Malcolm; he will be coming back with me- that, I can promise you."

Liz, followed by Colin, barged into the village police station – a tiny building with a small reception area, one interview room, and a filing office that covered as a staff room. That, with one small cell, was normally all that was required for the residents of Yetts Bank. Behind the police station was a small one-bedroom cottage which housed the resident police officer.

Now, with two extra officers assigned to the post, the place looked congested. The arrival of two irate people added to the sense of overcrowding. PC Hart sighed when he saw the irate couple enter the building.

Liz demanded to speak to Sergeant Burns, her anger clear for all to see. The young constable, unsure of procedure, attempted to stall her.

"The officer is interviewing a suspect, ma'am, and has ordered me not to disturb him."

"I do not want to know about your instructions. Knock on that door and tell him that Mr. Kent's aunt is here to see him."

With trepidation, the young constable knocked on the door of the interview room.

"WHAT?" hollered the senior officer, "I asked not to be disturbed."

"But, sir..." he began. Before he could splutter out any more nervous words, Liz pushed past him and stormed into the room.

"Aunt Liz!" said a relieved Malcolm.

"Madam," the sergeant said, "this is an interview of a suspect. Please leave immediately or I shall have you forcibly removed."

The young constable gulped at the prospect of having to handle the irate woman. He quickly returned to the main desk for safety.

"This is my nephew," Liz said calmly. "He had nothing to do with the dogs' death. I demand you stop this interview and release him. You either charge him NOW, or wait until his lawyer arrives. I'm going to call him."

As she reached for her phone, ready to punch in the number of her lawyer, the young red-faced constable arrived once more at the door.

"What now, Hart?" screeched the senior officer. "What part of don't disturb me do you not understand?"

"Sir," mumbled the constable, "there's a woman here, the postmistress, who claims that she made a mistake and wants to retract her statement. She claims that Malcolm Kent is innocent."

"Lord protect me from these villagers!" said the irate officer, as he stood up and headed for the door. Turning to the constable, he said, "Make sure no-one leaves the room until I clear up this mess."

Jessica Morris stood at the desk, her face ashen, and mumbled about getting her facts wrong.

"Sergeant, I misunderstood what he meant when he said it was all his fault. I realise, on reflection that he was in terrible shock at what he had discovered and felt guilty that he hadn't been around to protect the dogs. Please let him go. I am so sorry for troubling you."

"Madam," the sergeant replied, "you have caused me immense trouble. I ought to charge you with wasting police time."

Sergeant Burns returned to the interview room and hastily apologised to Malcolm Kent for his wrongful arrest.

"It appears that the local gossipmonger of a postmistress got her facts wrong. You are free to go, with my sincere apologies. No ill-feeling then, young man," he said, as he shook hands with the bemused youth.

Malcolm had no time to reply, as Liz intervened to vent her anger on the officer. "No hard feelings? You have not heard the last of this, Officer. Come on, Malcolm, let's get you out of the damn place."

Sergeant Burns, furious at the turn of events, spoke to Constable Bob. "God help you, Bob, having to deal with these crazy villagers. I don't know how you put up with living here in the sticks. I thought we were about to clear up one of the crimes in this confounded place, but it looks like we still need to find the poisoner. And as for that Ford vehicle, it's brought nothing but trouble. Stolen treasures indeed! That writer has a vivid imagination. Oh, get me back to the big city with real crimes to solve."

With that, he took off to return to his room in the guest house, hoping that the busybody landlady would be out and that he could have an early night.

∞∞∞∞

Door-to-door enquiries did not at first reveal any more information about either the poisoning of the animals or the black vase conundrum. A breakthrough eventually came when forensics matched fingerprints found on the vehicle to those of Ralph Harrison.

"Sir, I have a match," a forensic scientist called to his senior officer. "We have fingerprints going back some time to a minor traffic offence by Ralph Harrison, who was driving the vehicle in question, the Ford van. The prints were held on record, as were the details of the offence committed in Berkshire, not a stone's throw from where one of the robberies took place."

"Good work, James. That should get us a step nearer to solving those heists."

"There's more, sir. His prints match the one taken from the earring that was found on the van. There was a partial print, but enough to get a match."

The information was passed on to the investigators.

Meanwhile, the new owners, hardly settled in their new house, were distressed to be informed by the authorities that they might have to vacate the property to allow a thorough search to take place. Julie, passing by the Harrisons' home, saw Mary in the garden with the children. She had obviously been crying.

"Mary," Julie called from the gate. "Are you ill? Can I help?"

"Oh Julie, please come in. It's absolutely awful. We've been told that the police will be coming to search the house for stolen goods. They may have to rip up floorboards, after all the work that we've done to the house. Raymond is so angry. We are beginning to think that we've made a bad move by coming here."

"Oh, surely not. They can't rip up floors, can they? From what I know from my friend whose family was robbed, the police expected the stolen items had been sold abroad. Why do they want to come here? You poor dear."

"I don't know what's going on. Just as we thought we were settling in, this has come as a real blow."

That night Julie tossed and turned, upset by the plight of the lovely young couple. Sleep evaded her. Suddenly, she sat bolt upright in bed, her head buzzing with the thought: *the attic!* That's where they need to look: *the attic!* She remembered an earlier conversation with Jessica Morris at the post office when she had related how she often she'd seen a light on in the Harrisons' attic. *I wonder? Could it possibly be the answer?*

Julie could not sleep for excitement, and counted the hours until she could contact Sergeant Burns.

PC Bob was just opening the office, ready to start a new day, when Julie rushed in, breathless and excited, and with a request to speak to the sergeant. The constable sighed.

Attempting to keep calm, he replied, "Sergeant Burns will be along shortly. Meanwhile, can I be of assistance?"

Julie was about to suggest that she preferred to wait for the sergeant when the man appeared in the office, having recognised Julie's bicycle. He cussed inwardly, *not that confounded woman again? Not at this time in the morning, surely?*

"Good morning, Sergeant Burns, I'd like a word with you please about the robbery connected with the Ford vehicle."

Can't a man get into his place of work before being accosted by an excited villager? He thought. He forced a smile and showed Julie into the interview room, leaving the constable shaking his head as he continued setting up the office for the day's work.

"Sergeant," Julie began, "I think you should ask the fraud team to investigate the attic at the Newton's house before they start pulling the place apart. I'm sure the answer to the heist might well be found there."

"You want me to have the attic open and checked out? Do you know what rubbish people store in such places? If mine is anything to go by, there will be nothing of interest there. Now, what reason can I give the investigators to do such a thing? As I told you before, I need facts, not fairy tales."

Julie swallowed hard and ignored his remark. "I've remembered something that the postmistress told me some time ago, about how she often saw lights burning in the attic all those years ago when the Harrisons lived in that house. That was before Mr Harrison died."

As she spoke she thought how lame her reasoning sounded, and had no doubt that Burns would question her sanity.

"Um, Jessica Morris again? Hasn't she gossiped enough and caused enough mayhem in this village? Do you really want me to put in a request to open and search an attic on the word of a known tittle-tattler who remembers a light burning in a room forty or something years ago? Can you imagine the reaction that I'd get from my superiors? I would be laughed at by every copper. Sorry, miss, but you need to bring me something more realistic than an old dear's memory."

"Sergeant Burns, I'm not as mad as you probably think. It seems to me that if the vehicle was indeed used in robberies, no matter how long ago, the first place to investigate is surely the premises where it was located. If there were stolen goods in that house, the new owners would have found them by now. After all, they turned that place upside down during their renovations, including replacing floorboards. You want facts? I know for a fact that they have yet to open the attic; they were leaving that to the last area to tackle. They want to turn it into a play area for the children.

"If the investigators plan to upset the house and then find nothing, in all probability they will then look at the attic. Why not start there and perhaps save the family unnecessary upheaval in their property? I know Jessica Morris is a gossip, but she may be right on something. Have you anything to lose by my request? I could, of course, contact Lord Smythe-Watkins for his take on all of this, since his country house was one of the places where a robbery took place."

The sergeant stood up and guided Julie towards the door to indicate that the interview was over, "I don't think you need to disturb the gentleman. Leave this with me and I'll see what I can do."

He thought to himself that if there was a remote possibility of solving the crime, he would be a step nearer to returning to the city. *Maybe she has something here.*

Some days later, the Newton family left their home to allow a team to open their attic and look inside.

"We will be as quick as we can, sir," the chief officer told Raymond. "We'll cover the hallway in dust sheets, and cause as little upheaval as possible. Hopefully, we only need to have a quick look in the loft area and you and your family can get back home."

Raymond nodded in agreement, knowing that the sooner the search was over, his family could settle to normal life. The family were to be accommodated in the village hotel for the duration of the work. The children were excited at the prospect of being in the pretty building that they had often passed – a quaint, cottage-style building with thatched roof, bay windows, and a profusion of hanging baskets. It was a quiet time of year and the hoteliers agreed to provide accommodation and meals for as long as deemed necessary by the authorities. They were glad of the custom, and fussed over the children, making them special treats to eat.

"We are having some renovation work done to part of the hotel. I hope it won't disturb you too much. We will try to keep the noise to a minimum," the hotelier said. "This is normally a quiet time for us, and we need to refurbish some of the rooms to be ready for the start of the tourist season."

While it provided everything that the family required, it was upsetting for the Newtons to have strangers wander around their home.

"Goodness knows what they will find in that loft," Raymond said.

Mary said, "Probably loads of rubbish that's been gathered over the years, just like my parents' place where everything was stored. *It might come in handy someday*, my mother, the hoarder, would say." Mary smiled as she recalled her childhood days. "I suppose the only good thing is that we can focus now on turning it into a play den for the girls. Maybe they will clear the attic out, like they did with the garage." She laughed at the thought. "Meanwhile, let's make the most of this cosy place. I don't think the workmen here are too noisy, and they finish early enough for us to settle the girls for the night and try to keep to their bedtime routine."

A team arrived at the Newton's house and surveyed the area to be worked on. "There's a pole here for pulling the ladder down," said the foreman in charge of the operation, "so let's get going. Get this place open for the experts to check out, and hopefully we can finish the job ASAP."

Two men lifted the heavy pole, and with great difficulty attempted to place it so that it hooked onto the clasp on the attic door. They tugged. Nothing happened. They continued to tug at the hatch. Nothing happened.

"Pull harder!" shouted his workmate.

"This is impossible. We need more light up here so I can see what's stopping the hatch from opening. Oh no! Look at it, it's been bolted down. We need to have something stronger for us to stand on to prise this open, and something to unfasten the bolts. Why has it been bolted shut?"

Fraud officers, standing by to investigate the attic when opened, had to wait a bit longer for the area to be made secure. Scaffolding was required. The foreman called his office, "We need tower staircase scaffolding for this job – the type with a platform for the men to work on to loosen those darn bolts, and floodlights. This hall light is inadequate."

"It's going to take a few days to locate scaffolding and have it delivered to you," was the response.

"There's not much else we can do here until we have it in place. I'll send the men off to another job and recall them when we have the stuff," said the foreman.

The village buzzed with excitement at the activities at the house. Jessica Morris was beside herself with frustration. Since the incident with Malcolm Kent, she'd had to curb her gossipy tongue – something she found very difficult to do. Instead, she watched from her shop doorway as workers hurried back and forth carrying various tools. A few days later, a truck arrived to deliver scaffolding which they took into the house.

I bet that's for them to reach the attic, mumbled Jessica to herself. *I always knew there was something suspicious about that place...what with lights burning night after night...*

She watched from the safety of her shop window as heavy-duty pipes, tubes, and ladders were carefully taken indoors to erect the staging. The noise attracted the attention of a few villagers, who gathered to watch proceedings, but were soon moved on by officials. Once the staging was safely in place and the floodlights turned on to light up the darkness of the hallway, work began on opening the attic hatch.

The retractable ladder had been bolted at the hatch area by Ralph Harrison to prevent anyone having access. With several massive bolts in place, it ensured a difficult task lay ahead of the workforce.

"This is going to be more difficult than we thought," exclaimed one of the workers. "These bolts have rusted beyond belief. I can't move them."

Another worker attempted to remove the bolts, but again with no success. Others watching proceedings offered suggestions.

"Can you drill round the bolts to loosen them?" suggested another.

"Use an extracting kit," suggested another. "You may have to drill into the actual bolt. Centre it, don't bother about saving the bolts," suggested the foreman. "Just get the damn thing open. My neck is killing me, looking up there."

"Hand me up a vice grip," one of the men on the staging said, "I'll try that."

It was several hours before workers, taking turns to attempt the task, managed to loosen one bolt, which snapped as they tried to remove it. Language from the men on the platform was understandably ripe. They had taken it in turns to attempt the seemingly impossible task, oiling the bolts in the hope of releasing them. A specialist team from the serious fraud squad hovered about, ready to investigate the contents of the attic, should it ever be open.

"This could be a wild goose chase. What do we have to go on apart from some local person's gut feeling and a bit of gossip?"

"Our files remain open until the case is solved. These robberies were from way back, from posh country manors and the like. This might be the breakthrough that's needed..."

Their conversation was interrupted by a shout from the platform.

"Got one out, and another. Hey, boss, the whole damn thing is coming loose. We need another pair of hands up here. The hatch frame is solid; it's too heavy for us to catch."

With as many men as deemed safe to stand on the platform, tugging and pulling at the last few bolts that seemed determined to hold onto their secret forever, the bolts finally gave up the struggle like the embers of a dying fire, and the entire attic door loosened.

"This damn door is too heavy to move. Send ropes up, and we'll attach them and try to lower the door down there to you guys. Be ready to catch it."

With ropes safely attached and bearing the weight of the solid door, the men on the platform manoeuvred it off the staging. Those below waited as it swung precariously before landing with a thud in the hall passage.

"Got it!" shouted the foreman, "all clear."

"Oh, my God," cried one of the men from the platform. "You should see what's in here." He poked his head into the now open space and gasped in awe.

"Move over, let me look," said another. "Jeezo!"

The men were ordered down from their perch and asked to wait quietly until Chief Inspector Gates, head of the fraud team, climbed up to investigate the open, floodlit space, before climbing down to address the workmen.

"You chaps have done an excellent job. That was a mammoth task for you, and the Force is grateful for your assistance, but I must warn you that this is a crime scene going back several years. It is imperative that you do not talk about what you have seen here, and I mean to no-one – wives, lovers, drinking buddies. No-one must leak any information; no pillow talk, zilch, until I give permission. Do you understand? If you do not comply with this, you will face arrest. I know you are itching to reveal what you have discovered, but hold fire until I give you the nod to talk about it."

The tired workers looked at each other in surprise, but nodded their heads in understanding and acceptance of one of the most bizarre jobs they had been called upon to do.

∞∞∞∞

The Chief called his specialist fraud team to join him. They carefully mounted the scaffolding and stood together in amazement at what they were seeing. For a few moments, no-one spoke. All that was heard was deep intakes of breath as the team surveyed the attic area.

It was a large area; the three men could stand upright with headroom to spare. They stood on what appeared to be an expensive Persian rug that covered most of the floor area. Eventually one of them spoke, almost in a whisper, as if stunned at what he was seeing and afraid perhaps that some ghost from the past would appear and remove him from this staggering, secret place of intrigue.

"Well, I'll be dammed! I fully expected to find a creaky, dark, dingy place full of discarded crap...but this, oh man! We had best not touch anything; we need our forensic photographer here ASAP to record everything. Take care climbing down, chaps, we need to cordon this area off as a crime scene."

The Newton family were informed that their house would remain out of bounds to them for some time, until the attic had been thoroughly investigated and emptied of its contents. Unfortunately, no information was being released for the time being. Raymond and Mary, well settled in the cosy hotel, sat by the log fire discussing the strange events surrounding their new home.

"Who would have thought that a simple move to a lovely village would hold such a mystery? This is something to remind the girls about when they are old enough to appreciate it."

"But what on earth have they found in our attic?" asked Mary. "I'm truly mystified as to why the DI couldn't tell us anything."

"It sounds serious. Look at those guys, loads of them, dressed in protective clothing to process a crime...and in *our* house! You are right, Mary, it is intriguing. What do you think is in there?"

"Gosh, it could be anything. I hope it's not a body...I shudder at the thought that we shared our home with such a thing, harmless or not."

"Whatever it is, it must be important going by the activity over there. I think we would have smelled a body, don't you?"

Frank Summers, the crime scene photographer, had been a valuable member of the team for thirty years and was due to retire at the end of the month. With his usual efficiency, he photographed the scene in minute detail without disturbing any evidence. His photographic evidence would be an accurate record of the astonishing find. Having finished his work, he glanced around the attic and took one more panoramic shot, before being joined by DI Matthew Gates.

"That's my work done here, Matt. I've photographed everything."

"Thanks, Frank, have you ever seen the like of this?" Gates asked of his lifelong friend.

The men stood at the entrance to the attic and stared at the scene in front of them. The room had been set out as a private art gallery – a comfortable fortress full of stolen items, from expensive Persian rugs used as wall and floor coverings, to several small antique tables on which rested rare artefacts including antique brooches, several Victorian era cameo shell brooches in gold frames, many pieces of rare jewellery, rubies, diamond rings, and exquisite antiquities. The haul was astounding. Rare books sat on a rare, tiny, oak Credence table. Precious vases, table lamps, pictures and prints – decorative plates, too – were exhibited with care around the attic room. Two small comfortable Victorian walnut chairs were placed together, with an antique drinks table to hand. Other valuable items were in boxes, as if awaiting exhibition space.

"Those folks certainly knew how to make life comfortable for themselves as they admired their loot," DI Gates said.

"Matt, what's that book over there? I almost missed it.

There's so much stuff here," said the crime photographer. He reached in a corner for a hard-backed notebook that he handed to his superior, who perused the leather-bound book with utter disbelief.

"Good Lord, Frank! It's a detailed record of all the country houses that they visited, photographs, dates, details of what they took, and comments on the quality of each item. It's a diary of some sort. Good God, they have handed us evidence on a plate. Look at this entry: *'This tiny diamond is a replica Hope Diamond, an exquisite blue pendant that has a history of a curse. I felt good in it but did not want to wear it for any length of time due to the curse. Ralph tried to sell it in London but was offered only a fraction of its worth.'*

"We need to call in an art specialist for help with this haul. Goodness knows the value of what's in here. Let's get out, Frank, and make way for officers to begin the task of tagging and bagging items. I've never seen anything like this."

∞ ∞ ∞ ∞

Officers were keen to trace the children of Ralph and Belinda Harrison. Enquiries showed that their daughter – also called Belinda – had died some years previously. Her brother, Charles, was located in London, where he worked in banking. He was mystified when contacted by DI Gates to arrange an interview.

"It's regarding your previous home in Yetts Bank, sir," said the officer. "We would like to talk to you about your time there."

"I'm intrigued, Officer, as to what this is about. My wife and I were last at Yetts Bank when my mother passed away. We arranged to have the house cleared and put on the market. Everything went ahead with the sale of the property, and as far as I'm aware there has been no comeback from the new owners."

"It's not about the house sale, sir. That is all in order. Something else entirely. I'd prefer to talk to you face-to-face."

An interview was arranged, and the curious man arrived with his solicitor, should the latter's presence be necessary. Charles Harrison was a fine-featured man who carried himself well. His mop of thick hair showed a mere hint of grey and, with his trimmed moustache, gave him the appearance of a distinguished person. His blue eyes emitted a brightness that could pierce the soul of the onlooker. He radiated the confidence of a man at ease with himself and with the world. His handshake was strong and firm as he was introduced to the investigating officers and introduced his solicitor.

"I'm intrigued, Officer," he began, "as to what this is all about. I've brought along Paul Alexander, my solicitor, in case his assistance is required."

"I'm sure it won't be necessary as this is more an informal interview to clarify something about your time in Yetts Bank. I can assure you that you are in no way in any danger of requiring Mr. Alexander's assistance, but he is very welcome to sit in and observe proceedings. To begin... firstly, thank you for coming here in response to what must be a mystifying request. All will be revealed in due course. I'll start by asking you, if you will, about your memories of your life with your parents. In particular, about their working life."

Charles Harrison relaxed. Totally in control, he replied, "My mother was a homemaker, as they say nowadays – a housewife, as we would have then called her. She worked at home attending to household chores and all that it entailed, and spent her time writing letters, memos, notes of various kinds, and endless lists. She was never without pen and paper, and carried them in her apron pocket. It was a bit of an obsession with her. My sister and I loved receiving letters from her; they were so well written and full of news, snippets from the village, and from their travels.

"Father had his own plumbing repair service, and travelled around wherever he was required. My mother would often go with him for company, and in their spare time they loved nothing better than to visit stately homes. It became something of a passion for them. I hope this is relevant to whatever you have called me here for. We often felt that her literary talent could have been put to better use, such as writing a novel or two."

The officer said, "This is very helpful, sir, thank you. Do you by any chance still have those letters in your possession?"

"My goodness! No. I don't. I had a thorough clean-out of my things when I married, and recently we burned piles of paper when we were clearing the house, and a tin of letters that she had written but never posted. How on earth would my mother's correspondence interest you after all these years?"

"It was only a passing question, sir. Now, could you tell me something about the attic at home, were you ever in it?"

"The attic? Goodness, what an interesting question! No, we weren't allowed there. My parents told Bel2 and me that the attic was out of bounds for our own safety, as the area was only partially floored and they didn't want any accidents. They put the fear of God into us about children falling through floorboards with dreadful consequences."

"Bel2?" questioned the officer.

"Oh, sorry. I should explain...Bel2, my sister, was named after my mother, she was Belinda too, and as a child I called her Bel2 and the name stuck. Sadly, she was drowned on holiday in Spain when on a graduation party with friends. It was a dreadful shock to us all. Her body was never recovered, which made it all the harder to bear. My mother never accepted Bel's death, and in her fragile mind believed her to still be on holiday."

"Sorry for your loss, sir. To recap, you were never in the attic?"

The officer wrote furiously, causing Charles Harrison and his solicitor to exchange curious glances, then continued, "I understand that you and your sister were privately educated. That must have been quite a sacrifice for your parents, considering the type of work your father did. I say this with the greatest respect, sir. His business must have done well. Private education is not cheap. I investigated it for my son, but could not see how I could afford it on my policeman's salary."

Charles Harrison said, "Bel2 and I often wondered how they could afford the fees, and all the extras like school skiing trips and summer camps, and then funding us for university. When I asked my father about it, he merely laughed and said it has all been taken care of. We presumed that he had made some good investments. Strangely enough – and Paul here will back me on this – when my mother died and we were winding up the estate, there was barely enough money to bury her. Hence the rush to put the house on the market. Officer, please, what is this all about?"

"Of course. I'll put you out of your misery, but one more question before I do that... Did your father own a vehicle of any kind?"

"Only his trusty old Ford van that he used for work. It was

reliable, and he never needed to upgrade it. I left it in the garage with all the other rubbish that was there. It wasn't of use to me, and would be included in the estate. I couldn't locate the key for the garage and didn't relish the job of clearing out the area. Is there something significant about the old van that I should know about?"

The officer was silent for a moment, then reached for a book containing pictures of the contents of the attic which he opened and proffered to Charles. Paul Alexander drew his chair closer and both men studied the pictures.

"Have you ever seen these items, Mr. Harrison?"

Charles looked bemused as he replied, "No, never, what is the significance of these pictures?"

DI Gates, who had been silent throughout the interview, continued with the story.

"These items, artefacts, rare pictures, precious pieces of jewellery, etc, were found in the attic of your parents' home in Yetts Bank. We believe that for several years they travelled around the country robbing stately houses. The attic, as you can see, was set out as a private gallery."

Charles Harrison drew his hand through his hair, shook his head in disbelief, and for several minutes remained silent as he took in the enormity of what he had been told. DI Gates sent for coffee for the shocked men.

"I am totally stunned by this revelation. I presume you have proof of my parents' involvement?"

DI Gates explained that the evidence from the diary matched with the items discovered in the attic. He showed the diary to Charles, who confirmed the handwriting to be that of his mother.

"There is no doubt that your parents carried off several extremely clever heists without being discovered, covering a wide area, over a five-year period."

"I am shocked beyond belief," Charles said. "That explains how Bel2 and I were sent to boarding school... So, there were no clever investments as we believed...we were educated on the back of crime! Thank goodness Bel2 has been spared this traumatic revelation. I am beyond being astonished. This is hard to accept."

Feeling more composed, he continued, "What happens now? Will this be made public? I dread my parents' name – and mine – being at the mercy of the media. I am chairman of my bank. Who is going to trust a banker whose education came from the misery of others; whose parents were criminals? This could cost me my job and cause distress to my family."

"I'm sorry for the situation that we have thrust upon you, Mr. Harrison. So far, the press has not sussed this out, but it won't be long before they do. My team will be visiting the various country estates to inform the owners of the situation. All I can offer you is an assurance that the media are informed that neither you nor your late sister were aware of the heists."

A disheartened Charles Harrison and his solicitor left the police station. Over a meal which Charles pushed around his plate and barely ate, they discussed the momentous revelation.

"What I advise, Charles," said Paul, "is to take some time off. Make it clear at work that this is your annual holiday, and take Monica and young Rosie off on an extended break until the news has died down."

"My wife will be horrified by this, but I'm sure she will see the sense in going away for a time. Rosie has only a week left of the school term, so I'm sure she will jump at the chance of an early holiday. I'll think of some excuse for school, as I know they frown on the kids going off on holiday during term time. I'll explain it all to Monica tonight and we can talk to Rosie once we are out of the country. The older boys will have to be informed, of course. They won't want their university time marred by gossip. I'll give them the facts so that they can respond to any comments or questions that might come their way once the shit hits the fan."

"Yes, but warn them all not to say anything on social media, things escalate on Facebook and Twitter and such places."

The men parted company – Paul Alexander travelled to his office, while Charles Harrison headed home to come to terms with the knowledge that his parents had been criminals and how, in a few hours, his idyllic life had crashed around him.

∞∞∞∞

It took several weeks and many trips up and down the precarious scaffolding construction, before DI Gates declared the area almost ready to be returned to the owners. He asked them over to view the attic space and to explain what had been above their heads since they moved to Yetts Bank.

"Be careful climbing up here," he warned.

He showed them into the room, bare now of all its treasures, and produced a photograph showing the attic and its previous contents.

"Everything has been removed and we have a mammoth task now to trace the owners, that is, after the art specialist and forensic chaps have finished their work."

"Oh, my goodness," exclaimed Mary. "What a strange thing to have in an attic, a private art gallery!"

"Yes, but all stolen goods, I'm afraid. We now know that the vehicle in your garage was used for several robberies at stately homes throughout the country over several years, way back; about forty years ago. It's been a remarkable find, thanks to your local author and her sharp mind. Not to mention the local postmistress, whose inquisitiveness was of use after all!"

He laughed when Raymond added, "A nosy neighbour can come in handy at times!"

The inspector concluded, "The chaps will be here tomorrow with a new hatch door for the room, and to replace the retractable ladder that was damaged during the work. After that, the scaffolding will be removed, the place tidied up, and you good folks can have your home back."

Raymond said, "We were planning to turn the attic into a play area for the girls and were dreading the work involved, but your guys have done that for us. We've landed lucky, between having the garage and now the attic cleaned for us!"

"We aim to please our public," DI Gates laughed, as he took his leave of them. "I'm only sorry that we couldn't leave the beautiful Persian carpet on the floor, but it's a major piece of evidence."

"Oh, that would have been lovely," Mary said. "But we wouldn't have left it in the attic; it would have taken pride of place in the lounge."

An art specialist, John Shaw, who was part of the advisory fraud squad, was meticulous in his examination of the many objects found in the attic. His first task was to establish if the items were genuine, and for this he called in other art specialists to assist in the mammoth task. They divided the project according to the type of items. Months were spent researching each individual piece, taking notes as they went along, consulting and reporting their findings to each other.

With a final check, John Shaw – charged with overall responsibility – addressed a team from the fraud squad with his report.

"We have concluded that each item found in the attic of the house in Yetts Bank is the genuine article. No forged items were located, and we have estimated the total value in millions of pounds. Some of these itemised in this column," he said, as he pointed to a sheet of paper, "Are priceless."

He answered as many questions as he could from the incredulous squad and, satisfied that he had nothing else to report, packed up his belongings. His work completed, a fraud team coordinated by DI Gates then began listing the items against the information found in Belinda Harrison's diary.

"This diary is amazing," the officer said. "We've been handed essential evidence on a plate. Perhaps the writer intended it to be found when the haul was discovered."

Another officer said, "I expect you have something there. Or perhaps it was to salve the conscience. It seems that very few of the items were sold. The ones which were sold are listed here on this page, and seem to have been enough to fund their kids' education. The couple who lived here must have appreciated art but couldn't afford to purchase anything of worth, so they acquired things by theft. It's the strangest case I've worked on for a long time. Stealing arte-facts for appreciation...strange indeed.

"Yes, according to the diary, Ralph Harrison made a trip to Paris, met an art dealer – probably a rogue dealer – and passed on a few small items, enough for the Harrisons to live a reasonable lifestyle and send their kids to boarding school leaving them free for their 'hobby'. Nice work, if you can get it."

The next task for the authorities was to contact and visit the various country homes listed in Belinda Harrison's diary, to inform the owners – or, in many cases, their fami-lies – of the strange discovery of their stolen property.

"Some of these folks may no longer be around," said DI Gates. "Many stately homes now belong to trusts, who took over the running of the estates when costs became too expensive for all but the mega-rich."

His colleague replied, "My understanding of the situation is that if insurance companies have paid out, then the property legally belongs to the insurance people, who might or might not, offer to let the owners buy the items back."

"That could be troublesome for anyone who might want to have the goods returned. If these were mine, I would want them back."

Among those contacted was the Right Honourable Smythe-Watkins. Jonny was delighted to hear of the find, astounded at hearing of the hiding place of so many treasures, and anxious to have as many things returned as possible. He owed a debt of gratitude to Julie, and intended to repay her for her help.

"I am particularly keen to have my grandfather's war medals returned. They meant so much to my late father," He told DI Gates, when the officer assured him that the war medals were safe and undamaged.

Jonny and Maggie perused the list of found items, and considered which ones to buy back.

"I have to speak to our accountant and solicitor and decide if buy-back is financially feasible. Obviously, I would like to have everything returned," he told his wife. "We have a lot to consider."

"Darling," said Maggie, "I'll leave that decision in your hands. After all, this happened long before we met. You and Hermione are the ones who must decide what to do. I knew Julie was onto something when she spotted the vehicle in her village. What a coincidence that was, the vehicle being stored almost under her nose."

"Unbelievable," Jonny agreed, "but then, nothing surprises me where Julie is concerned!"

∞∞∞∞

With the Newtons safely back in their home and D I Gates and his team no longer required, Sergeant Burns, PC Hart, and Constable Bob were free to resume their investigation of the poisoning of the animals and the mystery of the black vases. The feared seventh vase had still not materialised, and most villagers had accepted that it was, in truth, a legend that had got out of hand and that they had no more to fear. The presence of three officers had calmed their concerns.

Liz and her husband decided to reopen their business. After a fresh coat of paint in the kennel area, a clean-up and rearranging of the paddock, along with restocking food, blankets, and other items required for the running of the business, they restored the sign *Safe Haven* to its former place by the gateway. Before long, they hoped that the happy sound of rescue dogs would once more be a feature of the village outskirts.

Julie called over to visit and to inspect the new-look area.

"Well, Julie," said Liz, "I expect you will want to feast your eyes on the next batch of dogs when they arrive, or is it too soon for you to take on another animal?"

"Liz, I'm tempted, very much so, but let's wait until we return from the book fair. I don't want any distractions. I'm working on my talk and want to get it just right. I'm so happy you still want to come with me as my roadie, and that Maggie is going to be there, too. What a threesome we are!"

"I'm happy to tag along as your dogsbody," laughed Liz. "You know I enjoy your talks and don't mind lifting boxes upon boxes of books for you to sign. It's good fun! Every writer needs a roadie."

"You are a good friend. Isn't it kind of Jonny to pay for our stay in a hotel with Maggie? She is longing to hear my talk; she's never been to a book fair. I suspect that Jonny sees this as a thank you to me for helping solve the heist."

"Colin has some days to take off from work, so he intends to be around here to look after the place. We couldn't possibly put Malcolm through that again."

As they spoke, a furry object wrapped itself around Julie's legs; a tiny kitten scratched at her legs demanding attention.

"Oh, look at you!" she said, as she lifted the adorable black kitten, "Liz, are you rehoming cats, too?"

Liz laughed. "No. Colin found two kittens in a box by the side of the road; abandoned, by the look of things. He brought them home until he decided what to do with them. They have taken over and made themselves very comfortable, so I guess here is home. We've called this cheeky chappie, Jingles, and the other shy one, Shadow. They have already established that they are in charge, so the dogs won't have a look in."

A few days later, armed with books, posters, and the like, the women set off for the annual book fair. Jonny's choice of hotel was exquisite, spacious, centrally situated, and an ideal spot for three friends to spent time together.

As the event progressed, Maggie, stunned by the enormity of it all, confessed, "Julie, I feel so inadequate as a writer when I see thousands of book people here. My meagre offering to magazines is a drop in the ocean. I feel my work should be consigned to a dark cupboard. I'm a fish out of water."

"Maggie, now listen to me," Julie said. "Your work is good. I've often told you that. If it were otherwise, the weekly magazines that publish your stories wouldn't look at them.

You give those readers what they want, and they can't get enough of you. What you write is good: you have interesting characters, strong plots, and your command of the language is first-class. We've known that from school days, so less of the woe-is-me and get on with the writing."

Liz looked at Maggie and smiled. "Well, that's you told off!"

"Right," said Julie, "Now that we have settled that, I'm off to hear Edwina Conta talk about her first book that has recently been published. I feel it's important to support new writers. I'll catch up with you two later, probably in the bar."

The venue for Edwina Conta's talk was packed, so Julie was glad that she had purchased an online ticket before leaving home. The Spanish author talked about her earlier attempts at writing, her failures to have her work published, and her future writing plans. Despite her difficulties with English phonetics, her accent was pleasant to listen to. Julie thought that the woman must have spent many years in the UK, based on her command of the language.

Conta began to read an extract from her latest book – an intriguing chapter that drew the listener in and held their attention. She had been reading for about ten minutes when suddenly, the silence in the room was shattered.

A woman sitting near the back of the hall, stood up and shouted: "STOP! That is my work you are reading. You have stolen my writing. That is plagiarism; you have stolen and published my hard work. You are a thief!"

The distressed woman began to cry, with anger more than anything else. People sitting nearby tried to console her, but she repeated: "My hard work, my years of research and writing, all stolen by that woman. That's why I came along today. I had read an extract from her book in a newspaper and recognised it as word for word *my* work."

Security staff were quickly on the scene and escorted the weeping woman from the room. Meanwhile, Edwina Conta – red-faced and flustered – gathered her belongings and made to leave the venue. A security officer took the author by the elbow and led her out by a back exit to an office where she was met by the event organiser.

Julie arrived at the bar to catch up with the others.

"That must have been a very short talk. How did it go?" Liz asked.

Julie related what had happened. "Girls, I'm not at all happy with this; something is bugging me. Here, give me a hand. Google this woman and see what we can find out about her."

The three retired to a quiet corner and worked on their respective laptops and phones to gather information about Edwina Conta.

"There's nothing here, Julie," said Maggie, after a lengthy search.

"I can't find anything either," added Liz.

"It's unusual for a writer not to have something on social media. After all, that's where contacts are made. Liz, check Facebook; Maggie, check Twitter, please."

They immersed themselves in the project, knowing that Julie would not give up her inquisitiveness. If there was something to be investigated, Julie would continue until she had answers.

After a time, Maggie said, "Sorry, Julie, there's nothing to show."

Liz echoed that.

"I have an idea. Something has just struck me. I'll check it out." Julie rummaged in her pocket for her ticket to the event. "Ah," she said, as she typed furiously as if her, or someone else's, life depended on it. Her companions simply looked at each other, and shrugged their shoulders as if to say, *Julie is on the case, don't distract her.*

"What have we here? Okay, girls, back to the drawing board and look up Lucille Jane Bradford."

Julie continued to type, tut-tutting as she went along.

"I thought so," she announced.

"I've found that name here," said Liz. "A housewife from quite nearby, but nothing about her being a writer. It must be the wrong person."

Julie said, "No, I think this is who I'm searching for. I remembered that name from when I booked my ticket on the internet. That's who payment had to be made to. I presumed it was the business site, but I think she's a fraud. Look for a picture of her on social media."

Caught up in Julie's enthusiasm, the friends searched, tapped, and clicked furiously.

"Here's one on the web," cried out Liz, as she turned her iPad towards Julie.

"That's the woman whose talk I attended. That's her! That's Edwina Conta, aka Lucille Jane Bradford. Let me borrow that, please," she said.

Julie grabbed the iPad from her friend's hand and almost ran towards the main reception area, where she asked to speak to the event organiser.

"I don't think he is available. There's been a bit of an incident; most upsetting, too. Mr. Quadri is with someone now, attempting to sort things out."

"Yes," Julie's voice was clipped, her frustration there for all to see. "I was at that talk and it is imperative that I speak to Mr. Quadri. Please call him and say that I have something important to show him which will help clear up the incident."

The receptionist hesitated, but only for a moment. Julie's stern face gave her no choice but to put a call through to the organiser.

"May I have your name, please?"

"Julie Sinclair. I'm one of the speakers at this event."

Pedro Quadri answered almost immediately. "Ah, Ms Sinclair. I know who you are. A very informative talk, I must say... Now, you have something to tell me?"

"To show you, actually. Do you still have Edwina Conta with you?"

"I do, indeed. The lady is most upset, and claims the person who interrupted her talk was totally wrong and that her work is her own."

"Mr. Quadri, the woman who claims to be Edwina Conta is a fraud. She is neither a writer, nor is she Spanish, although she is an excellent mimic as far as accents go. She is a housewife from nearby, whose name is Lucille Jane Bradford, and she has been defrauding your customers who have paid to hear her talk. I have evidence on my iPad and I've researched her on the web. This pseudo-writer has served time in prison for embezzlement."

"My goodness." The organiser couldn't hide his surprise. "Please come to my office; the receptionist will show you in. I have never had to deal with anything like this in the ten years that I've been organising these events."

Julie rushed into the office, where a red-eyed woman dabbed her eyes and looked at the intruder. She reminded Julie of a young pup who knew he had been caught making mischief and had no way out of the impending telling-off.

Mr. Quadri introduced the women to each other.

"Edwina. Julie Sinclair, one of our esteemed authors, has brought me some disturbing information." He turned to

Julie. "Go ahead, please. I'm anxious to hear what you have discovered."

Julie opened the iPhone at the page showing Lucille Jane Bradford's picture and, without a word, showed it to the fumbling woman whose faced paled as she realised that her scam had been exposed. Guilt was written all over her face.

"There must be some mistake...that picture looks a bit like me, but it isn't me," blabbered the guilty woman.

Julie said, "There has been no mistake, madam."

She stared so hard that the poor woman, unable to return her gaze, stuttered as she said, "I...I really didn't mean any harm to anyone...I've always wanted to be a writer, but my work was rejected by several publishers...I saw this as a way to get noticed. I didn't expect the writer to be at this event... I'm sorry for the deceit."

She wriggled uncomfortably in her seat, looking around for a way to escape, but her attempt was intercepted by Julie who used her height to advantage and stood over the trembling woman.

"You won't be going anywhere," said Julie, "except to prison."

Mr. Quadri alerted security and had Lucille Jane Bradford supervised as she waited for the arrival of the police. He turned to Julie, thanked her for her observation and stood as if to show her out of the room, embarrassed that the organisers had not done their research properly. He prided himself on his efficient running of the event.

Julie, however, would not be moved.

"What about the wronged author, Mr. Quadri? Where she, and what are you going to do about her? She is rightly very upset."

Pedro Quadri became agitated. He wanted the incident to go away so that he could resume the event.

"Hum, I expect the lady in question will have her entry fee returned. I can send a letter of apology and perhaps some flowers."

"FLOWERS?" Julie screeched. "If you think a measly bunch of flowers will console a writer who has probably put hours of work and a very considerable amount of money into her book, you have no understanding of what this event is about. Your organisers should research the authors who apply to take part in the event. If you had done so, this unfortunate incident would not have occurred."

A furious Julie left the bemused man and returned to her friends, who were anxious to hear what had transpired. A buzz went around the venue as word got out about the blatant plagiarism, while security staff kept the guilty woman in the office until police arrived to remove her from the premises. The wronged writer, much relieved that she had been believed, thanked Julie and her friends before being escorted to the local police office to make a statement, accompanied by her publisher who had been in the building with her, supporting her and other authors whose work he had published.

"Well, Julie," said Maggie, as the friends sat together in the hotel lounge, "you always told me that book fairs were interesting, but this one has been an eye-opener for me."

"Me, too," chipped in Liz. "This has been the most exciting one yet. Julie to the rescue, once more."

∞∞∞∞

Liz arrived home to the sound of barking. Colin met her at the door, a wide grin covering his face. By his side was an adorable golden Labrador who excitedly welcomed Liz.

"Colin?" questioned his smiling wife, "I can't leave you for any length of time and you go and get yourself a dog! Tell all."

Still grinning, Colin answered, "Do you remember Mrs. Wallace from the farm? Her husband died a few months ago and the family had to sell the farm, as she couldn't carry on with it. She has gone to live with her son, and the flat he is in won't allow animals, so she asked if we would take Candy and find her a good home. Candy, meet Liz. Liz, Candy!"

"You beauty!" Liz said, as she fussed over the dog. "You can be our new mascot, the first of many dogs that need good homes, and perhaps you will help us to move on and forget the horrid crime. Talking of which, Colin, has there been any development while I was away?"

"I spoke to PC Bob the other day. He said that progress was slow, but ongoing, whatever that means. We need a breakthrough to solve this."

Such a breakthrough came sooner than either of them had anticipated.

Back home, Julie had resumed writing and, as was her way, she took long walks to mull over ideas. Residents were used to seeing her wander around the village at all times of day and into the evening. She particularly favoured night-time when most people had retired for the evening and she knew she would not be interrupted by villagers who wanted to chat. She loved her community and the people in it, but relished the peace and quiet to wander aimlessly through the quiet streets, seeking inspiration.

She noticed a few lights shining in some houses: *Beech Cottage*, where Sophie, a new mother was probably attending to her infant; *Earl's Way*, number six, where elderly Eddie Dawson's night carers attended to the terminally ill man while Edith his wife had some sleep; *Dyke Row*, number four, where Marjory Roberts, a poor sleeper, regularly watched television until she nodded off in her armchair.

Something caught Julie's eye and stopped her in her tracks. A light from PC Bob's cottage illuminated the kitchen area where she saw the constable working on what was to end the village's mysteries. He had failed to close his heavy curtains and, through the flimsy net ones, Julie stared in horror at what she saw. She returned home, determined to deal with the intrigue in the morning. Sleep evaded her that night... *well, who would have thought?*

∞∞∞∞

In the morning, Julie breakfasted with unhealthy speed and collected her bicycle from her cluttered hallway, upsetting the various items that blocked her access to the bike.

Once again, she cycled furiously towards the police station, ignoring the cheery greeting from Timothy as he delivered the morning newspapers. She was on a mission and no-one and nothing was going to stop the incorrigible woman.

She was annoyed to discover that PC Bob was alone in the office, as she had hoped to speak privately with Sergeant Burns.

"Good morning, Julie," Bob said rather annoyingly. "What can I help you with now?" He emphasised the word 'now' – something which did not go unnoticed.

"Oh, I want a private word with the sergeant."

"He won't be here until later this afternoon, he's been called to a meeting in town. Now, if you tell me what this is all about, we might be able to fix it without the need to disturb the sergeant. He's a busy man, you know."

"Thanks anyway, but it can wait," Julie said, as she rushed outside.

Crazy woman, thought PC Bob, as he set about the day's work.

As she cycled home, she almost collided with the young officer, Constable Hart, who was heading to the station. She was so frustrated that she failed to notice him.

"Oi, miss, mind how you go."

Julie apologised for her lack of concentration and chatted with the young man for some time. She wondered if she should confide in him or wait until the sergeant returned; he seemed an honest young man, eager to get on in his career and anxious to please the public. Julie felt that she could trust him.

"Constable Hart," she began. "I'd like to talk to you in total confidence – and I mean total. I don't want PC Bob to hear what I have to say, but I will want you to speak in confidence to the sergeant when he returns."

PC Hart, unlike the other two officers, admired Julie for her observations that had helped solve the forty-year-old heist. He found her an interesting person to listen to; she lightened up the otherwise sedate pace of Yetts Bank, and he was keen to assist her intriguing request.

"Go ahead. You have my assurance of total confidentiality."

"Thanks, Constable." She related her discovery to the young PC, who listened attentively to every word she had to say, remaining quiet and uncommitted until Julie had finished her amazing account.

"Officer, please believe me. I'm not the crazy, mad woman that your superior thinks. I know what I saw, and I know what has been going on in this village...oh...and another thing..."

Julie remembered something that had slipped her mind. She rummaged in her oversized pocket and produced the foul-smelling bottle that she had found weeks before at Liz's place.

"This must be investigated, Constable. I'll entrust it to your care. Please take care not to be overheard when informing Sergeant Burns of my findings, and don't be surprised if he dismisses it as poppycock."

Assured that she had the trust and confidentiality of the constable, Julie headed for home to continue with her writing while awaiting the return of Sergeant Burns. Her unsettled mind disturbed her concentration, as she kept thinking about what she had discovered. She was impatient to hear from the sergeant, but knew she had to hold back to allow investigations to take place. *That is*, she thought, *if he believes me.*

∞∞∞∞∞

A week later, word went around the village that Sergeant Burns had called a meeting, to be held in the community hall, to update the villagers on the recent events which were as yet unsolved.

When Constable Bob asked his superior officer about the impending meeting, he was assured that all would be revealed.

"I think the good folk of this village need us to show some progress, so I've called a meeting to give them the latest update," said the sergeant. "We can't have them thinking that we are sitting here doing nought."

"Have we anything to update them with, or will we be giving the standard comment about everything possible being done?"

"Let's just see how it goes, shall we?" replied the sergeant.

At seven o'clock, the hall was filled to capacity. Every resident, it seemed, had managed to turn out for the gathering, keen to know what – if anything – had been discovered.

"I bet there's nothing to report," whispered a villager. "They want us to think that they are working on the crimes. I'm sure they haven't a clue as to what happened."

Julie sat with Liz, Colin, and Malcolm, near the back of the hall. She had found it difficult to keep her findings from her friends, but she knew the success of her discovery was dependent on her silence. She had to let the officers do their work.

"What do you think this is about?" Liz asked her.

"I'm sure all will be revealed soon," Julie replied, her head down to avoid meeting her friend's eye.

"Julie Sinclair," said Liz, "You *do* know something, don't you? Have you got yourself involved in another case?"

Thankfully, before she could reply, Sergeant Burns called the meeting to order. After the customary welcome and thanks for attendance, he continued, "I know you are anxious to have the crimes solved. I refer, of course, to the poisoning of those poor dogs – a disgusting and inexcusable crime – and the mysterious appearance of the black vases which caused distress and fear among some of you."

"Yeah," shouted out one of the village men, "but have you found the scum who did it? That's what we want to hear, not your usual stuff about the case is ongoing. We want answers."

A few more disgruntled people joined in, and soon Sergeant Burns could hardly hear himself speak. A loud voice was heard, "Keep quiet, and let us do our work." No-one had heard the young constable raise his voice before, and they were stunned into silence.

"Thank you, Constable Hart," said the sergeant, smiling at the young man who was showing signs of maturity and confidence. Secretly, the sergeant had been impressed by the progress made by his young officer. Initially, he had regarded the lad as a bit of a wimp, until the young PC insisted quite forcibly that he listen to what Julie Sinclair had discovered.

During the unrest in the hall, PC Bob had remained uncharacteristically quiet. But only Julie appeared to notice.

The sergeant continued, "Now that I have your attention, let me continue. The reason I have called this gathering is to finally put to rest the crimes visited upon your village, and to draw everything to a conclusion tonight."

There was a gasp of anticipation from the audience as they waited for the sergeant to continue. He moved to the centre of the stage and looked towards his two constables.

"Constable Bob..." he began.

The audience, expecting their local bobby was about to speak about the atrocities, were in for a shock.

Sergeant Burns continued, "Constable Robert James Stevenson, I place you under arrest for the unlawful killing of twelve dogs by means of poisoning, and for causing fear and distress to the community by placing black vases in their midst. You have the right to remain silent..."

The remainder of his 'rights' was lost in a gaggle of gasps and disbelief, as people tried to take in the enormity of what was happening. Liz turned to Julie, "You knew about this, didn't you?"

"Yes. I couldn't say anything, despite the temptation to do so. All will be explained in a minute."

Sergeant Burns raised his voice and the meeting came to order, as everyone stared at the downcast face of their local constable – a man they had known for many years, their very own friendly village bobby – and waited for an explanation.

"Constable Hart, cuff this man."

The disgraced constable allowed himself to be hand-cuffed, knowing that his career was over, his pension lost, and that he was facing certain imprisonment. As he was about to be led off-stage, a lone voice called out, "For God's sake, man, explain yourself to us. You owe us that at least."

Jessica Morris could not resist the opportunity to have her say. "I always knew there was something criminal about that man. Imagine him placing poor Malcolm Kent under arrest for something he himself did. Shouldn't be allowed..."

Bob looked at his sergeant for permission to speak to the assembly, and was granted a few minutes to offer an expla-nation to the stunned community that he had served for most of his career.

He mumbled, "I am truly sorry to have let you down. I never meant things to get so out of hand. I didn't mean to kill the animals; I only meant to drug them for a few hours, but I must have given them too much stuff. That's the honest truth. As for the black vases, no real harm was done. I only wanted to cause alarm in the village so that central office would send me assistance, instead of telling me that they intended to close the office and move me elsewhere. I was only thinking of you people... I didn't want you left without a police presence."

"Enough," shouted the sergeant. "Take this man away. There's a car waiting outside to remove him from here."

Sergeant Burns mopped his brow. This had been a diffi-cult night for him. He abhorred bent cops and hoped he never had to encounter such a man again, a man who was entrusted to care for his community, not destroy it or abuse his powers. The villagers were clearly stunned. Some were in tears as they thought of the man whom they had trusted with their very lives over the years, a friend who had turned on them. They wanted more explanation from the sergeant.

When he raised his voice, the meeting once more came to order. Everyone stared at the downcast face of their local constable as he was led away, then waited for a fuller explanation.

"Sergeant Burns," came the voice of Tom Carson, the community chairman and a voice of authority among the people. "Can you fill us in with more detail? We are anxious to know what has happened to cause this upset. This had been a dreadful revelation."

The sergeant drew up a chair and, glad to be seated, began his explanation of how the culprit had been caught.

"We owe it all to one of your own – a woman whose powers of observation and inquisitive mind has helped us in the past. I refer, of course, to the solving of a forty-year old heist. Julie Sinclair, on one of her evening walks, observed PC Bob at his kitchen table. The constable had omitted to shut his curtains, and Miss Sinclair saw him painting a vase with black lacquered paint. She quickly put two and two together and spoke to PC Hart about her suspicions. He in turn reported her findings to me and, on the pretext of sending Bob on a lengthy errand to town, we searched his house.

"Miss Sinclair had also come across a bottle of poison at the site where the animals were killed, and forensics confirmed that it was the poisonous substance which was found in the body of the animals. We found two more such bottles and a black vase drying off in Bob's kitchen. We had enough evidence to hang the man. Among our findings was a letter dated from three years ago, telling him that the village police office would close within the next few years because crime was minimal, and his services were required elsewhere.

"It seems he began this black vase nonsense to create a series of crimes, but things got out of hand when he poisoned the dogs. I genuinely think that he only meant to stun them. I'm sure, ladies and gentlemen, that more information will come out in time, but for the moment we thank our local author for bringing this to a close."

Everyone turned to where Julie had been sitting. But she and her friends had quietly slipped out of the hall, and were sitting in Julie's house analysing and discussing the stunning news.

∞∞∞∞∞

"I'm sorry, folks, that I couldn't say anything about my discovery. We couldn't risk PC Bob getting a whiff of it, or Liz going at him like a mad-woman."

Liz replied, "I probably would not have been able to hold back my rage, you did the right thing, Julie. You probably saved me from being arrested."

"What I don't understand," said Malcolm, "is what possessed him to turn from our well-loved local bobby to a criminal?"

"We left the meeting tonight before you heard what the sergeant had to say," said Julie. "But during his search of the police house, he and PC Hart found the evidence they needed, along with the black lacquered paint and a black vase that had been newly painted and left to dry. Oh, and I forgot to tell you that I found a bottle of poison in one of the kennels a few weeks ago when we were clearing up. Forensics said it was the same substance that was found in the dogs' bodies.

"A letter from police HQ – dated some three years ago – announcing that due to the low crime rate in Yetts Bank, the police station would be closed within the coming few years, resulted in Bob panicking and planning how to create some crime and request assistance to solve it. He was scared that he would be moved elsewhere. He made a dreadful error of judgement."

The others, amazed at what was being revealed, listened attentively as Julie continued with her account.

"The sergeant found an article in a magazine in Bob's kitchen, with a story about a legend of the black vase, and it obviously caught his imagination and began a route that was to be his downfall. He carried it off for two years – five vases, followed by six, and then this year it looked like he was going to produce the seventh one, which would have caused mayhem among the residents."

Colin said, "I can understand the reason for his actions that distressed the residents, but didn't harm anyone. But killing the animals, that was inexcusable, as was arresting Malcolm."

Malcolm took up the theme. "Do you think he really meant to kill them, or was it a ploy that got out of hand? Perhaps he meant only to stun them."

"We may never know the answer to that, Malcolm," replied Julie, as she poured wine for her friends. "I would like to think that he didn't meant to kill them, but who knows?"

Liz said, "What a sad end to an otherwise unblemished career. And to think that it was all so unnecessary. When the Newton's moved into the village, sooner or later they would have wanted to renovate the attic. The artefacts would have been discovered, and extra police would have come then."

"Yes," laughed Colin. "But thank goodness we had Julie on the case."

∞∞∞∞∞

Now that the Yetts Bank crimes had been solved and justice served, Sergeant Burns began packing for a very welcome departure from the village. *I'll be glad to see the back of this godforsaken place*, he thought, as he whistled cheerfully and closed his luggage. The police house had been thoroughly cleaned by some willing villagers, and awaited its new resident. A decision had been made at head office to continue a police presence in the village for the foreseeable future.

A phone call from HQ interrupted the sergeant's reverie. The Chief Constable congratulated him on such fine policing that had brought a bent cop to justice and reassurance for the residents of Yetts Bank. He finished by saying, "You have done a remarkable job there, so well in fact, Sergeant Burns, that I have decided to leave you in charge until such times as we decide what to do about the office. It shouldn't be more than a couple of years until we close Yetts Bank police station. You can move into the vacant police house immediately. Constable Hart will return immediately to his former post."

THE END

ABOUT THE AUTHOR

Terry H Watson qualified in D.C.E. and Dip. Sp. Ed. from Notre Dame College, Glasgow and Bearsden, and obtained a B.A. degree from Open University Scotland.

A retired special needs teacher, Terry began writing in 2014 and has published a mystery thriller trilogy: CALL MAMA, SCAMPER'S FIND, and THE LECI LEGACY.

She has written a compilation of short stories: A TALE OR TWO AND A FEW MORE, and a children's book: THE CLOCK THAT LOST ITS TICK AND OTHER TALES.

This latest publication, a mystery novella – A CASE FOR JULIE – will be followed by JULIE TAKES A BREAK and A LETTER FOR JULIE.

Terry welcomes reviews for her books.

You can contact her at:

Website: https:// terryhwatson.com

Twitter: https://twitter.com/terryhwatson1

e-mail: terryhwatson@yahoo.co.uk

Facebook Page: https://www./fb.me/RamoanPress

Lightning Source UK Ltd.
Milton Keynes UK
UKOW06f0302131117
312645UK00004B/23/P